How I Adore You

How I Adore You

ℑ

EROTIC STORIES

BY

MARK PRITCHARD

CLEIS
PRESS

Published in the United States by Cleis Press Inc.,
P.O. Box 14684, San Francisco, California 94114.
Printed in the United States.
Cover design: Scott Idleman
Text design: Karen Quigg
Cleis Press logo art: Juana Alicia
First Edition
10 9 8 7 6 5 4 3 2 1

For S., K., and especially C.

ACKNOWLEDGMENTS

Thanks to my writing coach, Sara Miles, who is also my best friend, and to Katia Noyes and other writers and friends who gave me their encouragement and feedback. I gratefully acknowledge three ongoing San Francisco institutions that have helped shape my erotic life and that of many others—San Francisco Sex Information, Good Vibrations, and the Lusty Lady Theater—and one that has passed into history, Queer Nation: These institutions gave me and thousands of others the opportunity to think, talk, and write about being perverts. Thanks also to the folks at Cleis Press; the Christian retreat center, which shall remain unnamed, that unwittingly provided me the setting where I finished these stories; Angela at the Muddy Waters Café on Church Street in San Francisco, where I did significant editing; and above all my partner, Cris Gutierrez, whose faith in me and love for me I feel every day.

Contents

Lessons in Submission

FOR O.

1

Go in the bathroom, take a shower, and wash your hair. Dry your body and comb out your hair, but don't dry it. Put your clothes back on so that your hair hangs wet and limp on your shoulders, dripping water all over you.

Come down the hall to the bedroom and stand before me. I'm sitting on the bed waiting for you, the low sun behind me in the window, blinding you to me except for my dark silhouetted form on the bed, leaning back on my hands. I'm staring at you, with the knowledge I have showing in my eyes that you can't see. You can squint against the sun, but the most you'll see is the glow of the light behind my blond hair. While you stand there waiting, you might wonder how to take a picture like this, the camera showing you what you can't see: my body hidden by a robe, my eyes boring into you, the strips of cloth in my hand.

I tell you to put your hands behind your back. It makes you look submissive, and to further enhance the picture I tell you to put your head down. Now all you can see are the splotches of water running down the front of your red silk shirt. I've told you not to wear a bra, and your left nipple is under a wet spot and it gets hard and pokes out, and the sleazy association that this is like some wet T-shirt scene is enough to embarrass you and further enhance your submission.

Listen to me: "You look delicious like this. Your hair is beautiful when it's dark and wet, and it's probably making you a little uncomfortable to stand there dripping, which just turns me on, because I want to make you uncomfortable enough to make you realize you've lost control. I want you to stand there and drip like this because it's how I like to imagine your cunt: so wet that there's come dripping off the hairs. You're probably standing there thinking this isn't so hard, to stand there and let me look at you, but just think of how many things I've already taken away. You can't see me; you can't touch me. You can't use your hands, and you can't go anywhere. You can't answer me or say anything. You just have to stand there and let me stare at you and talk to you.

"In a minute we'll go on and you'll realize just how little control you have, but for now, enjoy your freedom. Okay, you can look at me again."

Raise your head, but it doesn't do any good, the sun is still blinding you as it sets outside your window into the ocean. You feel the water dripping all the way down into the waistline of your jeans, where it stops and spreads out along your soft belly. Other rivulets have rolled off your shoulders and between your shoulder blades, under your arms, or directly onto the floor. You can shift your weight and step directly into a small puddle. The instant of imbalance from the water under your feet is enough to remind you that it's me, not you, who is controlling your slide into submission.

The sun sets, and you look straight into the orange ball as it balances on the horizon. Let it hypnotize you while you listen to my voice telling you the different places I'm going to put my tongue, telling you I'm going to penetrate you in places you never considered were possible points of entry. You're used to thinking of the cunt, the mouth, and, in really uncontrolled moments, the asshole. And boys have put their tongues in your ears. You didn't like it then, but I don't do that anyway.

What I do is stand up and unbutton your shirt and slip it off your shoulders. It hangs down from your waist and from your hands, which are still held together behind your back, not by any instruments but simply by your willingness to learn something about submission.

"I'm going to make you talk," I say. "At first it'll be easy. All you have to do is say 'yes.'"

"Yes."

"Are you my lover?"

"Yes."

"Do you submit to me?"

"Yes."

"Do you love to be with me? Do you relish the sound of my voice, the weight of my hands on yours? Do you desire me, strong and solid, next to you?"

"Yes."

"Do you think about my prick going crazy in your cunt? Do you think about licking the sweat from my body? Do you think about my leg going between yours when we kiss in public?"

"Yes."

"Are you ready to submit to me? Will you do what I say? Will you be brave?"

To everything you answer yes. Your voice goes through an interesting change—it gets deeper and fuller and connected to the desire that's in the burning center of your body—a desire that, at its deepest, has nothing to do with me, a desire that started when you were a child and imagined submitting to someone stronger, an older girl, a character in a story, anyone who understood your need to have control and responsibility taken away and replaced by her will. You were Scout, and Gregory Peck gently put you over his knee and spanked your butt as you told him your sins, things he already knew but you only become good again if you tell him. It's that voice I want, the voice that's naked and uncontrolled, the voice that knows the desire to fuck and the desire to get fucked are the same thing, that knows there's nothing bad about needing pleasure or giving up control, that only the strong have something to give up in the first place.

"Yes. Yes, yes, yes." You swallow, and with every word you look scared at first, then relaxed as you give it up.

You have a lot to give up. I really want it. It's this transfer and acceptance of desire that amounts to your submission.

Your skin burns orange in the light. Even if you look away for a minute, you see spots. The sun is too low to hurt your eyes but bright enough to intoxicate and hypnotize you with its brilliance. The whole room seems to burn with light that gets more and more intense; then in the space of a few moments it disappears. You are still blinded by the image of the fiery red ball, so you can't see me lie back on the bed and open my robe and masturbate while staring at you standing there blind and helpless.

"Close your eyes," I say. It doesn't matter, you still see the sun. Water is still dripping from your hair, more slowly now. "Open your pants. Open the belt, the top button, and the zipper. Pull them lower on your hips so I can see your cunt hair. Lower than that. Just high enough for them to stay up." I look at you and stroke my cock. "I'm having a fantasy," I say, "about jacking off onto your belly, so that the come runs down into your pubic hair and gets caught there. I comb the come into your cunt hair until it's coated by my come, so that instead of smelling like cunt you smell like sperm. It's another way of taking something away from you, of colonizing your body, so that you don't even smell like yourself anymore."

I get up and walk over to you holding a strip of cloth. My cock is hard but you can't see it because your eyes are closed, the image of the sun still imprinted on your corneas. "Put your hands at your side," I say, and go behind you and blindfold you with the strip of cloth.

"Would you do that?" I ask. "Would you wear my smell on your cunt…let's say, to work?"

"Yes," you say.

"Tell me you'll wear my come on your body whenever I want you to."

"I will," you answer.

You have to say more than that now. You have to tell me you'll do everything I say, and you have to tell me in detail and use hyperbole and go beyond what I've said. You have to show that you're turned on not only by the images of what we're talking about, not only by the fact that what you're saying expresses your desire as well, but also by the sheer fact that saying dirty and taboo things to me, these words coming out of your supposedly clean mouth, amounts to a further loss of control, to a deepening of your submission.

Example:

"I want your come on me. Shoot it on me, put it on my belly, on my face, on the lips of my cunt. Smear it into my wet hair, let it become part of me. I want your smell on me so that I'll belong to you, so that as long as I wear it before it washes off, I'm yours, as if you needed a sign, as if you didn't know I'll do what you want."

I need to hear this from you. Not only to make you do things but to make you admit to them. There's something about the voice that's more intimate, more alive than the body itself. The voice can do things the body can't. If I do something to you, you can always pretend later that it wasn't really what you wanted, but if you ask for it in advance, if you beg for it in the most imaginative language, if you use that voice that comes from deep inside your desire, then it reveals even more than your actions. Don't think you can fool me, either. You may be a good actress but I know the difference between somebody telling me what I want to hear and the real expression of need and desire that amounts to confession, which is another word for submission.

After I blindfold you, I stand behind you and reach up and touch your nipples. You aren't allowed to relax and lean back against me, so no matter how weak in the knees you get, you have to maintain your balance.

Now you can push your pants down farther—they fall around your ankles—and touch your cunt. The rule is that you have to tell me whatever it is you're doing as I stroke and pinch your tits.

"I'm parting my cunt lips. They're already wet, not just way inside, but all the way out, even the outer lips have come on them. They're hot and slick; I love the consistency of my juice at this time of month. Now I'm touching my clit. I'm holding it between my thumb and forefinger and stroking down along it like a prick. Now I'm pushing my finger underneath it so that I can rub myself—*ugh.*"

You can't do it so good that you can't talk. You have to be able to tell me what you're doing. You have go slowly enough and do it softly enough to maintain the narrative. What I'm getting from you isn't your hand; what I'm getting from you is your voice.

"My clit is hard. I—" You pause and gasp. "I like touching it with my two fingers pressed together like this...."

Don't stop talking.

"I'm rubbing it. I can't stand it. Yes I can.... Just don't stop. What you're doing to my nipples is driving me crazy.... I'm rubbing my clit—I'm rubbing my clit—"

I make you stop. Put your hands at your sides again. I keep touching your breasts. The nipples are as hard as pebbles of glass. You imagine them cutting my lips.

I lay you down on the bed, and you go on masturbating as I watch. You don't have to talk while you do it. You just have to show it to me. This is the first time you've ever done this in front of someone else.

You stroke yourself. As you get closer to coming, a secret escapes your lips and makes you come. After your orgasm you keep your fingers pressed against your pussy; the fingers of the other hand are unconsciously pressing against your breastbone, reaching in for your center of desire and selfhood that you are submitting to me.

I attach your wrists to chains. You begin trembling. I attach your ankles to chains. You become afraid. I put my hand on the spot you were pressing a moment before, and your fear stops.

You are splayed open on your bed. I start talking quietly to you again about how beautiful you are, about how much I desire you. You answer "Yes" again and again, like a mantra.

While you're tied there I kneel over your head and put my cock in your mouth. I penetrate you like that. I penetrate your cunt. I penetrate your asshole with my finger. I go back to your head and put my fingers in your ears while my cock is in your mouth. You can't see anything, you can't hear anything, you can't move, the only reality is my taste. My taste and smell and weight fill you, blocking out everything else. You aren't frightened, you don't want to get away, you submit.

2

It's dark except for the ceiling light, which casts a dim glow in the middle of the room. As soon as we walk in, I tell you to strip as quickly as possible. Then you get on your knees.

This is a pose you have to learn: Sit with your feet underneath you and your butt on your heels. This posture, used traditionally by the Japanese, has both humility and dignity. It's stable, and you can remain in this pose for a long time. But the best part about it is that, even though everyone can get into this pose for at least a few minutes, it becomes quite painful after a while, especially when you finally try to stand up and walk again. Yet it isn't dangerous; you can't really hurt yourself by remaining in this posture for thirty or forty minutes. Therefore, this act of submission will teach you about humility and pain.

As you rest like this on your knees, your legs are together. I couldn't touch you between the legs if I wanted to, not without your moving. That is not what is involved tonight.

When I bring in a bowl of hot water and a washcloth, you are waiting on your knees in the circle of light. I strip off my clothes except for my shirt, which I wear open. Wearing clothes while you are naked is intended to remind you of my power to grant you comfort and safety, or to take them away: to grant you pleasure, or to withhold it.

You have your head down. You can't see me anyway, not until I enter the light. As you kneel in the soft yellow glow, your head down and your hands behind your back even though I haven't told you to put them there, you look deliciously submissive, and I pause to stare at you and fantasize about how your mouth is going to feel on me.

I advance into the light and tell you to look at me. This is the first time you've seen my cock. Even if it makes you shiver, you look at it. It's the only chance you'll have to look at it for a while. I bring my body closer and closer until you are close enough to touch me with your mouth. Then I stop.

You lean forward until I can feel your breath. Then the first touch of your tongue, alarmingly warm, caresses the underside of the cockhead. Your tongue slowly circles the head, then you push up with the tongue so that you can lick down the underside of the shaft. That part of me is so sensitive the first time it is touched, and your warm mouth makes me tremble and groan as you work your way down to my balls.

Now your hands are gently touching my legs. You lean back slightly and take the whole cockhead in your mouth and wipe your tongue back and forth across the slit, tasting fluid. Your fingernails scratch slowly down my thighs. There is a mirror across the room in which I can watch you kneeling and sucking me.

You are allowed to bend forward as long as your butt is on your heels. That means I control how deep I go in your mouth. When I move forward, you take me deeper. When I move back, you gape at the missing presence.

I move forward again and tell you to touch my balls while you suck me, and to move your mouth rhythmically up and down. I can't tell you much, though; it feels too good. I'm touching my own nipples. After a few minutes, I'm already getting close to coming.

I pull back and ask you to talk about what we're doing. You describe the texture and taste of my prick, the sensation of being penetrated in the intimate hollow of your mouth, the enormity of my cock on your tongue. You also describe the pain in your legs and ankles and feet, the contrast between the spasms of pleasure you feel when you suck me and the pain and discomfort of kneeling to do it. You beg me to come in your mouth so that you can get the pleasure of my orgasm and so the pain will stop.

Oh, well, it's a false assumption that you get to change positions just because I come, but you'll find out soon enough. For now, beg me some more. I'm still touching my nipples. After a while the pain makes your voice frantic. I like that. I don't care if it's pain or desire that makes your voice quaver; you'll find out soon enough there isn't much difference.

I slip back into your mouth, and tell you to touch me everywhere you can, especially underneath the balls, behind the legs, and right before I come, my asshole. You pump me with your mouth. I don't really come very fast this way, unless you're awfully good at this. So this goes on for a long time. I don't know how to describe it to you except to say that, in addition to the pleasure I'm getting from you, the sight of you in the mirror sucking me excites me and helps me come.

As I get close, I start moaning and talking dirty. I say nasty things to you. It's one of the only times I've been really nasty to you so far, and I let it come out because it couldn't possibly be any nastier than shooting into your mouth. Gasping and shouting and calling you names, I orgasm, my hand leaving my nipple to slap your shoulder three or four times, a completely unplanned movement that leaves a hand print that lingers for an hour. Just as I finish, I thrust as deep as I can in your throat. It makes you gag, but I hold you there tightly for a few seconds out of pure selfishness. Then I release you and you have to cough.

When you can, you very properly resume sucking me gently to get all of the come. I touch your shoulder lightly, the one I slapped, and you pull off, pausing to kiss the very tip with your lips.

Sit back on your heels. You don't get to move. I bend down and hand you the washcloth, and you gently wash my cock, which remains hard for a few minutes. After you're finished you can wipe your mouth and chin, but I hope you've swallowed my come by now. I don't even want to have to tell you I desire it. You simply should do it.

I sit on the bed in the darkness and look at you. You're still in pain, but alongside the pain there is deep arousal, endorphins making you high and hungry. You ask me to slap your shoulder once again just where I did before; it was that slap, administered in the middle of everything else, that brought you over the edge from pain to pleasure.

What I really want to do is to slap your face, but I don't. That's for another time. I don't want you to move very much, either; it would mean taking your pleasure/pain away from you. So instead of hitting you, I tell you to part your legs and touch yourself.

Without hesitation you reach between your legs and bring yourself to orgasm, swaying back and forth and arching your back. After your second orgasm, and without stopping the motion of your fingers, you ask me to call you names again, so I do. In this moment, when you are all submission and desire and pleasure, you become the things I call you. This is not degradation, but music, when you are aroused.

After you come a few times, you need something else. You're swaying all over and about to rise off your knees, so I bring you over to the bed and pull you down over my lap, feeling between your legs from behind. I push a finger into your cunt, then quickly change it to two. I let you make all the noise you want, and you make a lot. Your voice is connected to your pleasure, and the sound follows your excitement up and down and around, uncensored, uncaring.

This is a picture of you in my arms, accepting pleasure and love, conquering your demons. This is the real you, strong and fearless, completely my lover. When we finally stop, I lead you to the mirror and turn you around so that you can see the image of my hand imprinted in your flesh.

3

We meet in public. You pick me up in your car and we drive south through downtown to an area awaiting redevelopment: vast expanses of churned-up land, old Quonset huts, rusting fences enclosing broken concrete slabs. We park behind an ancient, unused wooden warehouse.

We switch places so that you're in the passenger seat. I tell you to recline it, and to take off your stylish leather jacket. You aren't wearing anything underneath.

"This is so high school," you protest, pulling off the jacket and sinking back. It's quiet in the car, and with the seat tilted back you can't see anything except a corner of the second floor of the building outside.

I tell you to put your hands over your head. I pull out of my pocket two pairs of handcuffs, and with these I chain your wrists to the headrest. The *clickclickclick* noise as the cuffs fasten is loud, louder than the quick inhalation of air through your mouth or your heartbeat as fear pumps adrenaline through your system.

"You didn't do this in high school, did you?" I ask mildly.

"No," your shaky voice replies.

"I didn't think so. I think you should stop comparing what's happening between us with things that happened to you in the past. It's new, you know. You haven't done this kind of thing before, or been with someone like me, or felt what I make you feel."

"I know that, I just say those things to create an ironic distance."

"But there isn't really any distance, is there, between what you desire and what I know about you. There isn't any distance between my touch and what you feel; you don't have to process it through postmodernism."

"Actually there is a distance," you confess, "between your touch and what I feel. But I wish there wasn't."

"I know, we're working on that," I say, putting my hand gently around your throat. "Let's face it, you're completely tied up, and irony won't help you."

"All right, I'll shut up if you do."

"Sure," I say, and bend forward over your face to kiss you. Your lips reach out to mine, they're as soft and warm as lips have ever been. The small size of your mouth arouses me as we kiss, because I imagine pushing my cock into it.

Your kiss is delicious. I love the way you suck my tongue, the way I push deeply to feel the back of your mouth. You're so open to me this way that I kiss you for a long time, much longer than I usually kiss people, because it's here that your submission begins.

When I pull back from you, you remain open, arched, ready for me to plunge into you again. I push my fingers into your mouth, three fingers pointing together, then pull them out when you yank your head away because it was more than you expected.

There is a brief moment when you wait tensely for another penetration, then silence as you relax.

"So, you know," I say, "I really want to fuck your mouth and come in it."

You swallow heavily. "I know."

"Can I do that?"

"Yes, of course."

"Tell me."

"You're my lover, of course you can fuck me. It's what I want. I want to feel your cock in me, it doesn't matter where, my mouth is as good as my cunt. I want to feel your come shoot in my mouth, because we can't fuck without a condom and I want you to be able to do it in me." Your voice is low and soft, and your words come hesitantly. You're getting more used to talking this way, it's not as hard as it used to be. "When you come in my mouth, it's hot and sweet for me. I love the taste, I love the feeling of your uncontrollable fuck spewing into me. At that moment, it's mine, it all belongs to me. At the moment of your orgasm, you don't control anything. You give up."

"That's right," I grin. I like this dirtying of your mouth, you saying *fuck* and *come* and *prick* to me, your lover. It's not just the words getting your precious lips dirty, it's the very specific danger that the words could be closely followed by the acts they describe.

I gently lift the hem of your skirt over your knees. You respond with a little groan that is repeated again and again as I stroke your thighs. I touch you patiently between the legs, avoiding your cunt, coming close, making you imagine the places I'm not touching, the places where you dangle the cold metal of your own chains sometimes just to feel something hard and unyielding between the lips.

Your head has fallen back on the seat, and you're writhing gently as you remember the times my fingers have been deep in your cunt. Think how close they are now. Then the touching stops and you bend your body upward to receive it again, the same way you open your mouth to me after we kiss, like a thirsty patch of earth where water just sinks in and that never gets enough. Finally my touch is absent for so long that you open your eyes to see what's going on. I'm just watching you. I love looking at you when you're aroused. It's one of the main reasons I like to fuck you with my hand, to be able to do it and watch at the same time. I lock your gaze with mine as I put my fingers on your cunt lips and press gently inward.

Your cunt is wet; I never need lube at first. My two fingers sink easily into your body. I'm not pushing hard or forcefully, but your whole body convulses as I slide both fingers all the way in. It's one of the things your body knows how to do that you weren't aware of: how to move when it's getting pleasure. I push up against your G-spot to hear you draw your breath in, push down so that you can feel my weight against your body. You're sensitive enough to feel the callused places on my fingers, open enough to relax into the fuck. You love it this way, you're not getting too much, it's just right. You'll take it like this forever and come on my fingers over and over. Part of me says I should do this more often, I should get you used to my thickness. Another part of me says I should do this less often, make you yearn for it. I decide to do it a lot now, less often later, when you have grown to need it.

But I'm not happy just getting you to a trance-like place where you can get off; I want to stretch the possibilities of our desire. I pull my hand out and spread lube on three fingers and sink back in.

This is different than two fingers. Three is a lot wider, a lot less round, and it always hurts against the muscular vagina. There's something you should realize here: I like causing pain almost as much as I like causing pleasure, and I almost never do it accidentally. Giving pain and giving pleasure are two ways I have of expressing affection; I want you to learn how to feel one as the flip side of the other. Touch is a hot single, with pleasure a number-one hit; but when side A has played for a while and the nice people have had their fill and left the party, the rest of us turn the lights up a little higher and put on the B side, pain. With the lights up, pain reveals things that pleasure lets stay hidden.

But getting finger-fucked is an inefficient way to play with pain, because your cunt likes getting fucked too much and stretches; that's what it's made for, after all. I keep thrusting into you, though, because this is not just about pain, but about my penetrating you, my opening you, hurling my hardness and strength inside you. Your flesh gradually slides apart, admitting my fingers. Your cunt lubricates again, adding to the wetness, telling me what you're about to say:

"Please do that," you whisper. "Please don't stop."

"Don't stop what?" I ask instantly.

"Don't stop fucking me. Your fingers in me. Make me a province of your desire. I want to be the 'before' picture in all the self-help books about how to stop loving someone you're obsessed with. I want my friends to see the circles under my eyes and know we've been doing it for days. I want to take speed to stay awake for your tongue and your fingers. I want this to go on and on. Just keep fucking me."

I've been hard since I got into your car; I've been horny all the hours since I last saw you. Now your words are too much. I've got to get off. With my free hand I fumble with my jeans until they're down around my knees, I pick up the lube and squirt it on my cock, and then grab myself and jack off over your prone, spread-open, getting-fucked body. "Keep talking, slut," I hiss.

"I want your fucking hand inside me all the time. When I'm alone I think of how good you make me feel. I think of your hard obtrusive fingers fucking me, drumming on my clit, pinching my nipples and ears. I get that shaky feeling when I see your cock. You're showing me something I've never seen yet, you're masturbating over me…. Just don't stop pushing your hand in me, do it until I can take another finger, please, I wanna get fisted by you…. I know I can take it…. Oh god I think I'm gonna come—"

I come with a shout. My sperm flies out and lands on your naked thighs. You cry out at its touch, both afraid and greedy. Your cunt is spasming around my hand, I can feel it grip rhythmically, and it takes the utmost concentration to keep thrusting inside you to bring you the rest of the way to orgasm until you finally explode in convulsions. Your wrists pull against the cuffs, they rattle, and your voice is wailing loudly—suddenly the car is filled with noise.

When you finish coming, I pull my three fingers out and put two back in so you can relax around them.

Your eyes are scared and vulnerable, you don't know what to do next. At this moment, words fail us. I could tell you how I feel or how you feel to me or how fucking hot you look tied up with my fingers inside you and my come dripping off you, or that I love you and will do anything to make you do that as often as possible, but there's nothing to say, really, as silence settles back in, and the only sound is our startled breath.

You don't have to do anything. Now you're as open as I want you to be. I push into you again and you let out a completely involuntary moan. From now on there aren't any words, there is just thrusting and groaning and your body shaking around my hand. It gets dark while I fuck you, the windows are steamed up, we're perfectly enclosed and hidden and strangely warm. You can't see me anymore in the dark, just the shape of my body looming over you and the cool stickiness of my come drying on you. You didn't know there was this much pleasure. But if you opened to the pain, you can open to this.

It's simple: my fingers giving you pleasure; my eyes on you; you going deeper and deeper for each orgasm, back through dull gray years to a point when joy was yours. Connect the moments and you can keep this feeling: strong and loved, at home in your body, free in the world. When we finish and I finally unchain your arms, they are eerily cold and numb. You don't want to put on your jacket, you want to remain open and naked for me, but I insist.

As I start the car and we drive away, I tell you a secret. The warehouse is rigged. I broke in days ago and installed hooks, chains, and other accoutrements. We'll have to come back. But not tonight. You fall asleep as I drive you home across the bridge, cradled in the leather you bought to please me, dreamless and safe in the home of your body.

Ordinary Story

To Stephanie, 1968–1999

Just another white boy started talking to me, bought me a gin-and-tonic, danced with me, put his mouth around my ear, and took me home.

At first there was novelty, there always is. You start sleeping with somebody and you're fascinated with their neck, their hands, the curve of their belly, the way they kiss. Ron was a good lay and, on the positive side, rather tidy, without being meticulous. He always smelled pleasant, just on the good side of sweaty; maybe it was the laps he did every day in the pool after work.

But after I started shyly mentioning him to friends, I realized that Ron was, in addition to being white, American, tidy, and employed by the phone company, really quite ordinary.

Yes, being a good lay means (to me): He sucked cock very well, he fucked me and got fucked by me, he was a little submissive and a little toppy, depending on the mood, and he didn't look at himself too long in the mirror. He gave me pleasure, and I wouldn't ordinarily be pleased by somebody who was just ordinary.

But I had the hardest time putting my finger on something that really stood out.

The first person I tried to describe him to was Babs, the photographer downstairs. We ran into each other getting the mail, and when he mentioned he'd seen someone new around, I confessed that, yes, it seems we have a new boy.

"What's he like?" Babs grinned, leaning his long frame against the metal railing of the front steps.

I thought for a minute. "He works at the phone company."

"Oh, gainful," Babs said, pulling gently on his earring. "That's nice. But what's he like?"

"He's really nice. And he's a lot of fun," I said.

"Hmm, wonderful. We're really getting somewhere. I mean, what's he *like?*"

"Oh, about seven inches."

Babs sniffed. "Jizz, honey, you're the only man around who even tells the truth. I'm never gonna show you mine, you'll go around telling everybody what I really am."

"A slut, of course," I said. "No, I mean, he's really nice."

"You said that. It's a good thing he didn't steal your TV, 'cause you'd never be able to identify him."

"It's not that, it's just that he's a totally ordinary white boy."

"Oh, one of those."

"And yet, somehow special," I said thoughtfully. "I think."

"Well, baby," Babs said, heading up the stairs to his apartment, "you let me know when you find any distinguishing characteristics. I'm dying to hear it. Everybody has a secret, you know."

I went back upstairs. Only that morning, after Ron had left for work and I'd been at the kitchen table drinking the coffee he'd made, I'd been thinking about how good he made me feel and the hair on his legs and the perfect shape of his lips. Yet, on second thought, what was there to say about those things? He made me feel good and he has hair on his legs. I could be describing a horse.

His lips. Well, it's more like the *way* he kissed; there wasn't anything stupendous about his mouth, either. Nothing that would get him on television. And as for the way he kissed, it wasn't anything in particular....

I put the mail on the table, sat down in front of the computer, and started working on designing stationery for an architect who was opening her practice in the neighborhood. I'd noticed her with the real estate agent outside the building, made some comment, introduced myself as a graphic designer, and gotten the job. It was a piece of cake, and I was overcharging her even at the two hours' minimum.

His height, his weight: perfectly normal. Ron had some wonderful shoulders. That's one thing. I made a note and went on working. That's the thing about swimmers, they sometimes get pretty muscular; but everybody was muscular these days. You have to work out and be like the Joneses. I don't know how I escaped getting a tattoo when everyone else was.

His hair: brown like everyone else's, not colored or cut in any certain way or bleached, except by the chlorine of the pool. When I asked him where he got it done, he said he went to one of those fast-cuts places where some bored twenty-one-year-old who just got her license is experimenting with layers.

His eyes, hazel like a mutt's. Bright like a puppy's. Not particularly seductive. I started to wonder just what had attracted me to him that first night at the bar. I had found him standing next to me. I liked something he said but instantly couldn't remember what. It didn't matter, we started talking. I was just practicing, since I was really aiming to spear this kid who kept stopping people and saying, "Excuse me, but I don't think you realize I'm Michael Jackson." I was staring at his cocoa-colored skin and thinking about slinging him across my shoulders and throwing him onto the pool table and pulling his pants down. Then Ron put his hand on my shoulder and I decided to go with the flow.

A few days after talking with Babs, I was meeting Ron at a restaurant. I got there early and sat at a table facing the door so that I could see everyone going in and out. It was getting late and I was on my second drink when someone came and stood in front of me and said, "Hello, Jim, are you all right?"

It took me about five seconds of focusing on this specter, wondering who the hell it was while watching the door all the time for Ron, before I realized that it *was* Ron.

"Oh, dear. I didn't see you."

"No kidding. I walked in the door and you looked right through me." He kissed me.

"Sorry, I was thinking about something…. Um, how was your day?"

"Just an ordinary day," he said, sitting down.

"Don't say that—here's the waiter, would you like anything to drink?—you did something."

"No, really. What do you think working at the phone company is like? It's the same thing every day. I'll have what he's having," he added.

"Well," I said, taking a breath. Whenever I'm confronted with a conversational void, I launch into a total lie. "You know, I ran into someone."

"Who?"

"This guy I knew in college. Back then he had a reputation as a t-room queen. What do you think he's doing now?"

"Selling bathroom fixtures? Knee pads? Hair spray?"

"He's Elizabeth Taylor's personal secretary."

"Oh, is she in town?"

"She's launching her fragrance at Macy's."

"So did you have a go, for old time's sake?" he asked.

I laughed shortly. "No, he had to run," I said with finality, "and go help Liz. Well, would you like the fist, as usual?"

"I beg your pardon," he said mockingly. "Not while we're dining."

"The fish, oh my god, I meant—oh, dear." I sat there blushing and laughing.

"You're so cute when you fuck up like that," he said easily.

He's really rather masculine. Maybe it's his bisexuality. That's what I meant to make a joke about when I said *fist* instead of *fish* but it came out wrong. He has this girlfriend he still sees from time to time, although he says it's nothing serious. Someone he's known for a long time. I wonder if *she* thinks he's ordinary.

"Pamela," I said a few minutes later.

"What about her?"

"Don't you think I should meet her?"

He took a look at the salad on his fork. "Why?" he said.

"Or not?" I offered.

"Why not?" he countered.

"Well, I'm confused now. Let's start over. Would you like me to meet her?"

"So you can compare notes?"

"Of course, why else?"

"I guess I could invite you both over for dinner," he said. "Then I'd pretend I'd forgotten something and send you both out for it. Then you could compare notes in the car."

"You're so thoughtful."

"Great, we'll do it in a couple of weeks."

"Aren't you kidding?"

"No, are you? Wouldn't you like to meet her? I thought you said you would."

"Well, of course. What do you think about it?"

"I think," he said, "you'll have a lot to talk about."

᠎᠎᠎᠎ ᶾ᠎ ᠎᠎᠎᠎

"I finally figured out Ron's distinguishing characteristic," I told my friends Raz and Philip over dinner a few nights later.

"I know: He doesn't have a belly button," said Raz. "He's a space alien."

"No, it's that he doesn't exist," Philip said. "Jim's been single so long he's starting to think his reflection in the mirror is another person."

"You guys!" I said, shaking my fork at them. "I'm serious. I have to ask you about this."

"Sure, ask me, I'm an expert on white men," Raz volunteered.

"That's no surprise," Philip muttered. "Go ahead, ask Miss Milk Drinker of 1990."

"You are wrong!" Raz squawked, swatting Philip. "You are so wrong. Go ahead, honey," he said, turning to me, "tell Aunt Raz."

"It's that he has a girlfriend."

"You mean he is bi-sex-u-al? Oh, honey, Philip was right. They don't exist. You win as usual, Mister Meaty." They high-fived.

We were eating in the little Thai restaurant across from Does Your Mother Know, only steps away from the center of the queer universe, 18th and Castro. As usual, it was half-full, which still made the place, with its low ceilings and closely packed tables, seem crowded. There was another table with two guys, and a table up front with three Bears. The only other patron was an overweight guy in a dot-com polo shirt waiting for a takeout order.

"Is he bisexual on the way into the closet or on the way out?" asked Philip.

"He's not in the closet at all, he just has this girl he sleeps with once in a while."

"He tells you it's once in a while, but actually she's his wife."

"He is ly-ing to you!" hissed Raz gleefully. Raz would qualify as a typical black screaming queen, only he says everything in this Very Quiet Voice, as if it's all a secret. It just makes you lean in to listen to him, which I find very seductive.

"He is not married," I protested. "I've been to his place. He lives right up there on Corbett. He has the David refrigerator magnets and the campy greeting cards and a drawer full of old Queer Nation stickers. He got arrested protesting *Basic Instinct*. He's as queer as I am."

"Uh, Jim, I hate to tell you, but have you looked at yourself lately?" Philip said in a mock-serious tone. "I'm afraid you have…Gap disease."

Raz cracked up. They high-fived again.

"I don't see you flaming," I said to Philip.

"It's different for me. I am an Academic Type. Observe the tweed jacket."

"Philip is a pee, aych, dee!" Raz hissed conspiratorially. He liked saying this and managed to say it at practically every social occasion.

"In science!" exclaimed Philip in a tone of triumph, like that guy on NPR.

"Seriously, honey, what do you think a bisexual is?" asked Raz, trying to spear the tofu in his Pad Thai. "He's somebody who cannot deal with his own queer self and come all the way out of the closet. He wants to prove to himself and everybody else he's really normal, while every Friday night he's down on his knees at the Powerhouse."

"No," said Philip, "it's someone who wants the privileges of a straight lifestyle and the danger and excitement of queer sex, at the same time. He's really queer, but he can't give up his straight privilege."

"That's what I said."

"What straight privilege?" I asked. "I'm telling you he's not married. He lives alone. He files taxes as single. He does not take this woman home to mother.... At least I don't think he does."

"You see? You see? Look how little you really know about the man," Raz said.

"What do you know about how he files his taxes?" Philip said. "It's October and you've only known him two months."

"'The Double Life of Ron Whiteman,'" said Raz. "'Starring...Ron Whiteman.'"

"His name is not White Man."

"All right, you tell us what you do know. Who is this woman he fucks?"

"Her name is Pamela. She teaches literature at a private high school."

"Catholic school, I'll bet."

"Just a *private* school. She's from San Francisco. They met at a 12-step meeting. In the Castro!"

"Of course he met her there, he lives in the Castro."

"She volunteers at Maitri Hospice," I said weakly. "She drives a Camaro. I know what you're thinking! She is not a fag hag!"

"She couldn't be a fag hag if she fucks him. The whole point of being a fag hag is that you don't have to have sex with the men in your life," Raz said.

"True," Philip nodded, his mouth full. He high-fived Raz, who reluctantly went along, as if his analysis had not been worthy of a high five.

"Never mind about her, I'm trying to tell you about my boyfriend. Jeez!"

"Jim," Philip said, pointing his fork at me, "do you fuck him in the ass?"

"Yes."

"And does he suck your cock?"

"Yes."

"All right then—he's a fag."

"Yes, but a fag who goes both ways."

"Oh, you mean he fucks you sometimes. That's been known to happen," Philip shrugged.

Raz shook his head sadly. "Jizz, I'm sorry. What you have there is a garden-variety white fag. While certain specimens do show unusual behavior, I'm afraid this one came from a very common batch long after factories had been set up to mass-produce them."

"Ha ha ha!" Philip laughed. "*Antiques Road Show.*"

"I'm afraid he is worth, at most, twenty-two dollars. With the carrying case."

"I'm sorry I mentioned it."

"Next item!" Raz called out. The waitress came up.

"Something else?"

"Yes, dear, are there any bisexuals?"

"Hey? What that?"

"It's a kind of meat...that likes fish."

"Hey? No. No such thing."

"Thank you. In that case we'll have some more Thai iced tea, please." He turned to me. "Case closed."

֍

I should have known better than to consult a couple of dyed-in-the-wool sixes, but I didn't expect Ron's own reaction.

"I'm not bisexual," he said.

It was Sunday morning, and we were over at his place. The night before, just to make sure, I got him to fuck me, and then I fucked him. So far so good. Then I made him tell me his earliest experience with a man and made him jack off for me while he told me. Turns out the little jail bait had seduced his high school choir teacher in the rehearsal room. Then before he came, I made him tell me about his first experience with a woman, and I made sure he came when he hit the high point in that story.

That cinched it as far as I could tell. So the next morning over breakfast when I had said, "So how did you decide you were bisexual?" he said:

"I'm not bisexual."

"What? You have sex with women, don't you?"

"Just Pamela."

"Well, she's a woman, ain't she?"

"Yeah, but...I just want to make sure you understand: I'm not one of those self-hating fags who says they're bisexual."

"Well, what are you then?"

"I'm one of those self-hating fags who sleeps with women."

"Oh, come on."

"All right," he said. "Observe." He picked up his half of grapefruit and expertly divided up all the little sections using a special grapefruit spoon with serrated edges. "Voilà. But watch this." He picked up my half of the grapefruit, grabbed his ordinary coffee spoon, and sectioned the grapefruit just as perfectly. "There you are."

"Now my grapefruit will taste like coffee."

"Fine, we'll switch. My point is, only a fag would own a special grapefruit sectioning spoon, and only a fag would be able to perfectly section a grapefruit *without* the special faggy spoon. Need I say more?"

"But you fuck girls!"

He shrugged. "Nobody's perfect. I was kidding about the self-hating part. That's what some people say. Actually, I don't give a fuck. But if you're asking me how I define myself, it's as 'a fag who fucks girls.'"

I shook my head. "Well, there we are," I said.

"Have I passed the test now, Miss Lick?"

"Who's Miss Lick?"

"My fourth grade teacher. The biggest dyke who ever lived who never knew it. I blame her for my sexual confusion."

"Is it really confusion?"

"No, I'm kidding again. I like fucking men. I like fucking Pamela. I'm not confused about that."

"Okay. I'm sorry. I don't want to make you feel like I'm putting you to the test."

"Ha. You were last night. I haven't jumped through that many hoops since Miss Lick. She made us do long division in the mirror."

"No!"

"I swear. As if long division weren't bad enough for a fourth grader. She would write a problem on the blackboard, and we had to look at it in a mirror over our shoulders like Annie Oakley. Then we would tell her how to solve the problem verbally, 'Six goes into 25 four times, 1 remainder, 6 goes into 16 two times, 4 remainder—256 divided by 6 is 42, remainder 4!'"

"Good lord. What was she like?"

"Just as you'd imagine—she wore these wool A-frame dresses, like a Sears version of Coco Chanel, in beige or maroon. She had this close-cropped hair, salt and pepper. Flat shoes. Glasses with black frames. She was a butch, big time."

"Wow. Did she beat you?"

"You bet. If she caught you cheating on a test, man! With the blackboard pointer! In the hall!"

I reached out for his hand. "Oh, Rhett. Now I *do* see why you're so perverse."

☞

It happened the way that Ron said: He invited us both over to dinner at his house. I made the salad and set the table while a pan of vegan lasagna cooled and he grilled vegetables.

"Do you know what a vegan is?" I asked. "It's someone from Las Vegas who has not yet lost. Get it—Las—Lost?"

"That sucks so bad."

"That's what they used to be called: 'Las Vegans' or just 'Vegans' if you needed space in a news headline. I saw this in the Las Vegas newspaper when I was doing research there this year."

"What were you doing research for?"

"I'm writing a modern-day *Macbeth,* starring the Bing Crosby family, and called *MacBing!*"

"You are never eating here again."

The doorbell rang. "There she is. Get that, willya, doll?"

"Sure thing, sweetheart." I set my drink down on the kitchen cabinet and nervously padded toward the door. Ron lives in one of those weird Twin Peaks apartments that have fabulous views, but white shag carpeting. Every time I see white shag carpeting I think I'm on a porn shoot.

I opened the door.

She was six feet tall and wore a woolen car coat, beige with a dark fur collar. On her head was a beige felt pillbox hat, and on her feet were beige pumps. She wore cat glasses. She was Miss Lick.

"Holy cow," I said smoothly.

"You must be Jim," she said. "It's a pleasure to meet you, Jim."

"And you're Pamela. Oh boy. Please come in."

"Thanks so much." She was carrying a cake in a pink plastic container that I thought I recognized from the shelves of the AIDS benefit thrift store. At least I supposed it was a cake. She stepped into the apartment, wavering slightly on the thick carpet, but recovering quickly. "Is the lady of the house in?"

"Um, in the kitchen."

"Naturally." She strode forward. "Hello, there. Where's my sweetheart?"

Hey, wait a minute, I had just called him that.

"In here, cupcake!"

I trailed her into the kitchen, where they exchanged kisses on both cheeks. "Here's a little something," she said, handing the cake container to him. He handed it to me and helped her off with her coat. I put the cake on the counter, and he handed her coat and hat to me. Under her coat she wore a beige woolen dress with little dark-brown leather buttons and a collar with dark-brown piping. With her hat off, I could see she had long straight brown hair wrapped in a bun. It was like seeing a faded color photograph of your aunt dressed for an early Easter.

"How was parking?" he asked brightly.

"A bitch," she said, just as brightly.

"Have you met Jim?"

"I have, and he's chaaarrm-ing," she smiled. "How *do* you pick 'em?" She spoke in a superficially pleasant but somehow menacing tone, like a tightly wound movie star speaking to a maître d'. I didn't know whether it was meant be entertaining or hostile. If she were a guy in drag putting on the same act, I would just laugh. But I didn't know what to make of an actual woman doing drag.

"Coats can go in the bedroom," Ron suggested.

"Right." I tossed the coat and hat on the bed, then returned to the kitchen. Pamela was standing between me and my drink, and I decided I wasn't going to let her intimidate me.

"'Scuse me, that's my drink there," I said politely.

"Oh, this," she said. "Here you are."

"Can I get you something?"

"I'll have what Ron's having."

"I'm having what *he's* having."

"I can see I need to make another pitcher of martinis," I said.

"What's for supper?" she asked. "Oh boy, lasagna."

"Tell Pamela your joke about vegans, Jim."

"I don't think I can *milk* any more humor out of that one," I said.

"Ha! That's a good one, Jim," she said.

"It's much better than the first, lousy vegan joke he told," Ron said, hand on hip. "I'm disappointed that you were funny this time," he said to me.

I made the martinis, and Ron moved the food to the table. We commenced eating, sitting boy-girl-boy: me and Ron facing each other, Pamela at the head. It gave me a feeling that he was showing me off to her, rather than vice versa.

We made dinner small talk, and Pamela kept up the brittle movie-star tone. With a southern accent she could have been a Tennessee Williams heroine. But she grew on me, and by the time she had finished telling us the story of how she learned the tango from some female RAF officers at a club outside their base in Scotland, I was taken in.

What with the martinis and the wine over dinner, we were all feeling a little giddy by the time I cleared the plates. Pamela had decided to teach us how to tango. "It's very simple. All you have to do is count and walk backwards and forwards at the same time, along with your partner. I'm an excellent teacher, but let's all take our shoes off, shall we?"

She started with me and Ron dancing together to learn the first part of the basic pattern; she made me the girl, which I didn't mind all that much, but when she cut in and taught the second part, she still led, which meant that I was the girl again.

"Shouldn't I learn the boy's part too?" I suggested.

"It's a good idea, but learning both parts in one day is too diffi-cult, so I'd say you're stuck being the girl for tonight."

"That goes for all night," Ron put in.

"Great."

"'Great, *Daddy*.'"

"Oh, my," Pamela exclaimed, dipping me. "Now we're all learning something."

Ron danced with her next. Since he had danced the boy's part with me, he got to be the boy with her. I wasn't sure I liked how this was turning out.

"Now dip me," Pamela said. "Oh yes baby. Dip me harder. That's right. Oh, you play the man so well."

"Very nice of you to say so," he said in a fussy voice.

"Aren't there any more martinis? Jim, make some more, there's a good girl."

"If Ron's the man and I'm the girl, what does that make you?"

"Haven't you guessed? I'm the teacher."

Pamela put on some actual tango music and tried to get Ron to keep time with the music, but he wasn't fast enough yet, and they kept falling behind. She would count "One, two, three, slide four, aaaaaand *five* six seven eeeeeeight—and nine, ten, together. And *one*...."

"Oh dear," Ron said, stumbling.

"No, it's back, back, back for you, then slide."

When the martinis were ready, they were both a little sweaty and frustrated. He tried to dip her at the end, but she pushed him away. "No dips for a boy who can't keep up."

"It's this damn carpeting."

"That's not what you'll say later. Jim, maybe you'd like to try again." She poured herself a stiff drink and tossed a quarter of it off.

She strode up to me, all butch and woolen, placed her hand just under my shoulder blades, and pulled me roughly to her. I let out a gasp as I looked up to her bright red lipstick and cat's eyes. Staring hard at me, she removed the useless glasses and flung them away. Then in a completely normal voice she said, "Just let me show you how to move." Then in her teacher voice: "Ready...and *one*...."

She pulled me forward for the first three steps, then caught me in a balance for the pause, then we moved back for the next few steps.

"That's the way...together. And *one*, two, three, slide four...."

I found myself being steered by her as if I were a little sailboat on a white fluffy lake. I ignored the counts and just let myself be steered by her hand. Miraculously, we were dancing. She snapped at Ron to flip the music back on, and there we were, mincing and striding like—well, if not like Argentines, at least like decent students.

The song on the CD came to an end, and she dipped me so deeply I could feel the hair on the top of my head touch the floor. Then she snapped me upright for the last note.

She bowed to me like a dancer and, not knowing how to bow like a dancer, I gave her a little Japanese bow. She laughed and Ron applauded.

"Oh boy!" she exclaimed. "You didn't tell me he could dance!"

"He didn't tell me either," Ron said with a cocked eyebrow.

"It's just because of the way she leads," I said, happy.

"Teacher's pet." Ron stuck out his tongue.

"Now Ronald, that's not the way to behave," Pamela said, her voice thinly menacing. "We have ways of dealing with boys who are rude. And you can forget that 'Daddy' stuff for tonight, as well."

"Aw heck," said Ron, perhaps reverting to a fourth grader.

"One more word out of you, mister, and I'll give you heck."

"I just—" Ron blurted.

"That's it, mister. Clearly you don't understand who's boss around here."

I retreated to a bar stool and sipped my martini quietly, content to watch what came next. The tango CD was still playing. He stood forlornly, his face suddenly transformed into a boy's: fear, outrage, and excitement, mixed.

"Would you go kneel in the corner of the room, Ronald?"

He looked at her like she was crazy. Clearly this was something they had not negotiated in advance. But he went to the corner she had pointed to.

"Face outward, please. Good. Perhaps you can follow instructions. Can you follow instructions, Ronald?"

"Yes."

"Very good. You'll get your chance to prove it to me. James, come here, please."

I climbed off my stool and came over to her, standing next to and slightly behind her.

"Now James, I'm well aware you don't do girls, so don't fret, I'm not going to push you on that. Just be a good girlfriend and unzip me, not quick like it's a costume change, but pretending, for just a few moments, that maybe I'm actually a slim boy in really good drag with a cock underneath here that needs to get out. But slowly, so that Ronald can watch."

I reached up with shaking hands and unfastened the little catch at the neck of her dress, then unzipped her slowly, all the way down. Then, standing behind her, I gently moved the dress on her shoulders so that all she had to do was step out of it, transferring her martini from hand to hand as she withdrew her arms and let the dress fall around her legs.

She was wearing some very complicated underwear, a bra and garter belt and lace panties, and they were all bright blue with black trim: very Frederick's of Hollywood. Another bit of drag.

I folded the dress neatly on a chair, then turned around and looked at the two of them, framed in the square of the huge wall of windows that faced the city. Anybody with binoculars or a telescope—and I knew lots of people in these view apartments kept them at the ready—could watch our little play. "Should I close the blinds?"

"No, let the greedy voyeurs watch," she fairly cackled. She walked across the carpet to Ron, turned around, and bent over with a flat back, her hands on her knees. "My ass is dirty, Ronald. Clean it, please."

I stared as he went to work. She smiled up at me. "Ronald told me he was afraid you thought he was a little boring," she said. "Do you think Ronald is boring, James?"

I was going to say *Not anymore,* but I caught myself and decided to tell the truth. "Yes, I do."

"Well, you're ninety percent right," she said. "He is pretty ordinary. But I've known him for a long time, and there's always been a side to him that's, well, capable of surprise. Ah!" she caught her breath. She dropped her head to look for a second through her legs, then looked up at me again. "Usually he needs a little help with it. Don't you, Ronald."

"Yes," came a boy's voice.

"Are you happy to have my help, Ronald?"

"Yes, I am!"

"Good. Now you're doing a pretty fucking good job there, Ron boy…." Her voice lost the put-on quality for a moment, then she continued in her drag voice. "A pretty good job for teacher. When you're done, there's something else I'd like you to do."

I was getting a hard-on, and she noticed. "I see you're also happy with the situation, James. I'm glad. Here's what I'd like you to do. For many years, Ronald has promised that one day he would show me how he sucks dick. Would you let him show me, James?"

"Yes, Pamela."

"That's good." She reached into her crotch for a second, and it looked like she was going to masturbate, but she must have gotten a vibe from me that it would break the mood, so she pretended she was just adjusting her garter belt.

"That's very good, Ronald." She straightened up suddenly, causing him almost to pitch forward. She peered out the window. "Hello out there! One two three see me. Do you want to wave, Ronald? No? That's all right. Now come here, James. Come over to Ronald. Look how wet and messy his mouth already is. Would you like to make it messier? You would? All right. You just stand there. Make sure the nice people across the way can see. Just cheat out a little, that's right.

"All right, Ronald, the show's all yours. Open him up and take it out. But before you touch his dick, you have to say one thing."

"What's that?" he said, his hands frozen on my straining zipper.

"You have to say, and loud enough so the whole class can hear, 'Fuck your boy's shitty girl-assed mouth.'"

"Oh jesus."

"That's not what I said. Now you remember how you got into this predicament, by mouthing off? There are many predicaments worse than this, Ronald. Do you want to find out what they are?"

I kind of did want to find out what they were, but Ron did not. "Fuck your boy's shitty girl-assed mouth!" he sang out.

"Well done. Now he's all yours."

Ron tore open my pants and instantly shot his mouth down on my penis. I couldn't believe it. Usually he's slow and gentle and sort of technique-y; he does fine, but he always does it the same way. Now he swallowed my dick like it was the last one he'd ever suck. I felt my prickhead penetrate his throat, and still he jammed his head down harder, like he wanted to impale himself.

"Holy shit," I said weakly. Ron's hands were all over my balls, tickling them the way he knew I liked, and since he wasn't concerned this time about making me last, he sort of did it all to me all at once. Already I could feel a quiver at my core, and when Pamela knelt down next to him saying, "I want to watch you fuck him," having her in the picture was suddenly more exciting, not less.

"Oh man," I warned. "You're gonna make me come,"

"Oh call him 'bitch,'" she suggested scornfully.

"You're going to make me come, fucking bitch!" I said.

"Oh yeah," Pamela said. "Say it again." I realized she was masturbating now, they both were, way down there by the floor, but I didn't care any longer.

"Fuck you, bitch," I hissed. "Fuck you, fucking cocksucker, you fucking shitty bitch, oh gawd!" And a few moments later I started coming.

"Fuck you," Pamela hissed, right into Ron's ear. "Take his come, little boy. Get your mouth fucked by Daddy."

A groan came from deep within Ron's throat. Now he was jacking off, fast, and he emitted three wails that sounded more like the whinny of a horse. Pamela bent her head down to the floor.

"Get fucked by Daddy's prick," I hissed at him, the stuff squirting out of me. "Fuck you, little boy bitch, little mouth, drink Daddy's fucking come."

They both grunted loudly, sounding about the same. They both had cocks in their mouths now.

I bucked back and forth a few more times in Ron's mouth and then stepped back, pushing him away. He sucked in a huge breath of air, *hhhuuuuuuuuuuuuuuchhh!* and then wailed again, still coming in her mouth. I looked at the back of her head bobbing up and down in his lap, her hair bun bouncing like a brown ball.

Then she raised her head and kissed him, and I watched him suck the come out of her mouth. She finally sank back onto the carpet and rolled away.

I stood in front of the window, my prick drooping and dripping, and looked at my boyfriend. His face was smeared with come and lipstick and saliva, there were pubic hairs stuck to it, and tears were rolling out of his eyes. He sat back on his heels and tried to recover his breath.

I turned my head and looked out the window. About sixty yards away, on a deck that was cantilevered out over the canyon from a building that was slightly higher on the hill than Ron's, three guys were laughing, clapping, waving their arms. Through the glass I could just hear them yelling, "Wooo-hoooo!"

I sat down heavily on the couch and looked at Ron on the floor and Pamela, lying on her back, her knees raised and moving lazily in the air.

Then she spoke.

"Are you a big fag, Ron?" she asked in a completely normal California voice.

"Yes," he chuckled.

"What kind of fag are you?"

"A bisexual! I'm a fucking bisexual fag!"

"That's right," she said, smiling, her body rolling slightly from side to side. "Don't you forget it."

Cousin

The summer after I turned sixteen years old, when my family lived in a suburb outside of Houston, I had a little affair with my cousin.

Until she showed up with my aunt, I wasn't doing much that summer. I would ride my bike four miles to the pitiful suburban library, check out three or four novels, and carry them home in the wire basket. I would spend the rest of the day in the house reading the books I'd borrowed. The next day I'd do it again. There was nothing else to do. Oh, I also worked at the Jack in the Box on NASA Road. The less said about that, the better.

What I was spending my time reading were regular grown-up novels. Back then—in the mid-1970s—all the novels that were available at the Clear Lake library were about suburban people a little younger than my parents, having love affairs and swapping wives, and generally being sexual revolutionaries in a suburban Nixon-administration way.

Every single one of these novels had at least one dirty part; sometimes more than one.

Now, because I also spent a lot of time in those days thinking about Jesus, I was conflicted about how much I enjoyed reading the dirty parts of these novels. But I reasoned that it was perfectly natural for sixteen-year-olds to be horny and think about sex all the time when they weren't thinking about Jesus.

So that was what I was involved with that summer: riding my bike, novels about suburban swingers, Jesus, and Jack in the Box.

Then my Aunt Mary and her daughter Judy arrived. My uncle had died early that year, and my aunt and my cousin were sort of on the national tour of family members. They were supposed to spend two weeks with us.

Judy—or Crazy Judy as she was sometimes called in our family, because of her frequent and spectacularly unsuccessful suicide attempts—was sixteen years old, too. She was in a manic phase that summer. Instead of trying to commit suicide, she was extremely enthusiastic about everything. She wanted to go sailing, play miniature golf, and buy souvenirs of every place we went to.

My mother took them to the local sights—the Space Center, the San Jacinto Monument, the beach at Galveston. I tagged along because Judy and I were the same age.

After spending so much time just riding my bike and reading novels, I was glad to spend time with Judy. She was dumpy and I was a geek, so neither of us felt superior to the other, and since there was nothing else to do we started fooling around with each other. After all the adults had gone to bed, we would make out on the couch in front of the *Tonight Show*.

Each night we went a little farther, from kissing once or twice to tongue-kissing for fifteen minutes at a time to her taking her shirt off, to dry fucking, and finally, on the last night before she and her mother left, I succeeded in sticking my fingers far enough into her pants to actually touch her cunt. That was as far as I got, but it was pretty far for a scrawny, horny sixteen-year-old who didn't even have a girlfriend. I was ecstatic.

But the next morning she was oddly distant. Since we had started making out about ten days before, whenever we were together in the presence of our mothers, we would look at each other with these secret smiles. But on the ride to the airport, as we sat together in the back seat of the car, I couldn't catch her eye. And at the airport, she wouldn't pose with me for a picture.

On the way home, I felt deflated and resentful. She'd let me go so far already—would it have killed her to smile at me for one more hour? I wasn't going to french-kiss her in the car. I just wanted some acknowledgment of our secret. But she would hardly speak to me. After that, she never responded to a letter I wrote, and we lost touch.

I didn't see her for nearly twenty years. But that's not to say I didn't hear of her. In the early '90s she wrote a book called *Devil's Consort,* about her childhood subjugation by a satanic cult. In the book, she described how a small group of suburban Tacoma devil-worshippers had enslaved her at age three and made her their plaything. According to the book, her father had been one of the main culprits, her mother, my Aunt Mary, only a pathetic collaborator. The book described in detail the horrible rituals in which people and animals were tortured, raped, and killed, all in an oppressive atmosphere of scented candles and imitation wood paneling. Judy's book coincided with the rise of the afternoon talk show, and she became a minor celebrity and authority on matters satanic.

Even I was mentioned in the book. The way she described our adolescent groping was like this: I was "married" to her during a cult ceremony in which we had to drink each other's blood and then fuck on the altar, or ping pong table. Then she conceived and bore a son, who in due course was killed in the cult's ever more vicious rituals. The last mention of me in the book was as a "pornographer" who had moved to San Francisco and been "lost in that doomed city's maelstrom of sex and death."

Flattered as I was by this inflated portrait of my role in Judy's life, I never confronted her about it. Even though I had been mentioned by name, there were so many horrible incidents depicted in the book that I hardly stood out. The only contact I had with Judy was when I was home after a root canal and happened to catch her one day on *Sally Jessy Rafael*. She'd come a long way from the plain, manic teenager I'd made out with. She was done up like some queen of the talk shows—lots of makeup, purple silk dress, big hair, and one of those huge bows that women used to wear in the '80s. She was a sort of a cross between Tammy Faye Baker and Dianne Feinstein. There she sat, telling her story of how she'd been victimized by her parents and their bridge club.

And the other reason I didn't object to her portrayal of me was that I really was a pornographer in San Francisco. I was publishing a sex zine, and eventually brought out a book of sex stories, but for all my efforts to publicize my work, not very many people noticed it, and it could reasonably be said that I had, in a sense, truly been "lost in San Francisco."

Then the notoriety that sprang up around her book died down, as everyone lost interest in the satanic child-abuse thing, and I didn't hear anything of her again for some time. When I finally did publish my own book of smut, it made nowhere near the splash her weird fantasy had.

A couple of years ago, I found myself back in my family's old house in suburban Houston for Christmas, with my brother and his kids, and my sister and her kids, and me on my own, when who should call from the airport, asking if she could come for Christmas dinner, but Judy.

You can imagine that Judy was not very popular in the family since her book had come out. Her own parents were both dead by now, but every time the family got together during the late '80s and early '90s, the conversation eventually worked its way around to Judy and her book and how it couldn't possibly be anything but a figment of her imagination. This meant I never did have to explain to them about my being a pornographer in San Francisco, much less the satanic wedding she said I'd participated in, or my supposed devil's spawn offspring. They just assumed everything in the book was Crazy Judy's fantasy.

But it was now six or seven years since the book had come out. So when she called from the airport, my mother—who didn't make the book, and who could never turn away a family member anyway— set another place at the table and dispatched me to the airport to pick Judy up.

On the drive to the airport, all kinds of things went through my mind. What should I say to her? Should I ask her why she had written such a horrible book? Why she had lied about me? Had any of it had been true?

I found her outside the United Airlines baggage claim, sitting on a green army duffel bag and smoking a cigarette. At first I didn't recognize her. The big hair was gone—or not exactly gone: The big hair was now in blond dreadlocks past her shoulders. She had multiple piercings in each ear, in her lip, and in her nose. She wore a kind of Mad Max brown-and-white desert nomad outfit and giant black combat boots.

She saw me before I recognized her, because I'd told her I would be driving my mother's acid yellow Cadillac. She flicked the cigarette away, hoisted the duffel bag onto her shoulder, and flung it into the back seat. Then she hugged me and got in the car.

We headed home. "I read your dirty book," she said.

"Yeah, I read yours too."

"How come you didn't put me in your book?" she said. "I wrote about you."

"Yeah, well...." I didn't know what to say to that.

"You should have put me in one of your dirty stories."

I had to laugh. "Maybe I should have. But you obviously gained renown without my help."

"Yeah, all my renown. That's all over with." And she went on to tell me about finishing her college degree with the money from the book and going on to work in a Rape Crisis Center in Eugene, where she'd tossed the DiFi look and become a punk vegan. For a long time she was a celebrity among the women's community there for being so brave and exposing the satanic abuse cult, but after doing Buddhist meditation for a few years she'd fessed up and announced that she'd made the whole thing up. For this she was ostracized, so she moved to Berkeley, where she'd been working at a macrobiotic restaurant for the last three years, only a few miles away from me in San Francisco.

By the time she finished this story, we were home. My family—probably the last time they had seen her was in her talk show phase—was still expecting some kind of Dianne/Tammy Faye character. But there were lots of people in the suburbs who dressed like Tammy Faye, so when she showed up looking like a refugee from the cast of *The Road Warrior,* they were nonplussed and never really got their bearings back. But they did their best, even though there was no macrobiotic vegan entree and all Judy ate were the sweet potatoes and the salad. She and I sat next to each other at dinner, and everyone tried to make a lot of really bright, happy comments.

Afterward, we all went into the living room and gathered around the tree. Now, it was the custom in our family that my father would read the Christmas story from the Bible every year. But since he had died a few years before, my older brother had taken over. However, for some reason, my mother felt it would make Judy feel more part of the family if she read the story. When she asked, "Judy, would you read the Christmas story?" our jaws all dropped.

Judy took the Bible, opened it, and began reading. She started with the decree when Quirinius was governor of Syria, and did it straight—all the way to the point where Jesus was lying in a manger, "because there was no room for them in the inn. But the cows and the sheep shared their hay with the baby Jesus, and baby Jesus never forgot how nice the animals had been to him. For his whole life, he never ate meat, and all his disciples never eat meat either, because the animals had given Jesus their hospitality. And that's why all Christians to this day are vegans."

My brother's eight-year-old kid spoke up, "Daddy, are we vegans?"

"No," my brother said angrily. "She's not reading it right."

"How come we eat meat, Daddy?"

"Never mind," my brother said, taking the Bible away from Judy. "I think that's enough scripture for tonight."

At the end of the evening, after the kids had opened one present each and everyone else had gone to bed, Judy and I sat on the couch in the living room, the same couch we'd made out on. All the lights were off except the Christmas tree lights, and the *Tonight Show.*

Judy said, "I'm sorry I didn't write you back."

"You mean twenty years ago?"

"Yeah—you can imagine, though, that I was pissed, but it wasn't really your fault."

"Why were you pissed?"

"More because of everything else that was happening to me."

I didn't know if I wanted to go into that, but she just went on. "You know, what really happened."

"What did really happen?"

"My dad actually was molesting me. I mean, it wasn't all that satanic bullshit, but he was still fucking me. So the only way I could get out of the house for a while and stop him doing it was to stage a suicide attempt. Then they'd lock me up for a few weeks, and I wouldn't have to worry about dad sneaking into my bedroom every night.

"Then when he died, you wouldn't believe how relieved and happy I was. That's why I was such a spaz about everything when I was here that summer. It was like a weight had been lifted off me."

"So why did you write all that shit if it didn't happen?"

"Just to get back at him."

"But why drag me into it?"

"Oh, come on, Mark. I didn't make up that much."

"You mean, aside from our satanic wedding and you having my child?"

"No, I mean, about you being a pornographer."

"Well, yeah, but—"

"When we visited you that summer, I was just in a good mood, and you seemed really horny, so why not mess around? It was fun, right? You should have written a story about it."

I just shrugged. I kind of had to laugh.

"Anyway," she went on, "I thought after all these years it might be fun to see you. Here we are on the couch again. Do you want to fuck?"

"Jeez, I don't know," I said. "How do I know you won't turn me into some monster character in your next tell-all?"

She put her hand on my crotch and said, "We'll just have to see about that, won't we?"

Trick

He was short and solidly built. A little muscled, not like a gym queen with broad shoulders and a huge chest, just strong the way you would be if you grew up working. He did go to the gym, I found out later, but just enough. He had Asian skin but a black man's lips, Asian nipples but heavy, kinky hair on his legs. His head hair was pretty kinky, too, but he kept his head nearly shaved. His right eyebrow was pierced twice with little bars, as was the center of his fleshy lower lip.

What do I mean by Asian nipples? Of course, they aren't all the same. But a boyfriend of mine, who used to watch all sorts of porn, had these videos of Japanese and Chinese girls getting fucked. And a lot of them had these big nubbly nipples, whether or not their tits were big. They looked so chewy, so inviting, that I wanted to put them in my mouth. And when Cary took his shirt off for the first time, I saw he had them too.

I said, "Damn, you've got those great Asian nipples," and he was, like, "What do you mean?" I couldn't very well go into a long story about how I'd seen a load of straight porn videos, so I said something about how it was just my name for nipples like his.

Then I said, "Excuse me," and threw him on the bed. I jumped after him and put my hands on his shoulders and put one of those nipples in my mouth.

He made sounds.

Outside the motel room, you could hear the busy part of Lombard Street, a dull roar in the early evening as commuters headed toward the bridge.

He was only a college kid—didn't have much to say. On e-mail he'd been pretty outgoing, but when we met in a café, he wasn't. Guys that young aren't necessarily shy; they simply haven't been socialized yet. They let their youth cover all the charm they need. I thought he was a little boring, but since I'd invested this much time, I decided to go for it, and we checked into the Ocean Breeze.

He lay there in his khakis and let me lick his nipples. Touched my hair a little, made noises in his throat. I wanted to turn him on, draw him out, make me want me. I wanted him to tell me something, make a request, step out of the passive mode. My impatience kept me active but just in case, I made sure my crotch was within his reach.

I switched to the other nipple, licking, just licking.

He said, "Oh yeah."

"Oh yeah what?" I smiled.

"Just oh yeah."

"Does it make your cock hard?"

"Take a look for yourself."

So he could talk. I figured he just needed some cues.

"Why don't you tell me how hard it makes you, while I suck your tits?"

"It gets my cock hard, it feels good, like you're doing, oh, yeah."

"I like it when you talk."

That just made him laugh.

I started twiddling both nipples with my fingers. At this point I didn't have any clothes off. "Tell me a story," I said, looking into his face.

"What about?"

"I don't know, don't think about what turns me on, tell me a story about what turns you on."

He looked at me, then up at the ceiling. "I have a daddy. He's a little older. I suck Daddy's cock all the time. He calls me 'boy.' 'Boy, I want you to suck my cock,' he'll say. And I do."

"Tell me about his cock." I was starting to get hard. I love it when people talk.

"His cock is cut, nine inches, a big white fat cock. It fills up my mouth just right. He fucks the shit out of me and holds my head close and yells at me, 'Suck my cock, boy! Suck Daddy's big cock.'"

"That's great," I smiled. "You really have a daddy like that?"

Instead of answering, he reached for my crotch. "Let me see it," he said.

I got off the bed and dropped my pants, so that I wasn't wearing anything but a gray T-shirt and briefs. I climbed back on the bed and hooked my thumbs under the elastic. He lay there staring at my cock, grown hard under the cloth.

"You want to suck Daddy's big cock?" I asked.

"You're not my daddy," he smiled. "Believe me."

I chuckled. He put his hand on my dick and stroked it through the cotton fabric. "Let's see."

I peeled off the briefs, leaving my dick bobbing in the air. He put his hand on it. I steered it to his mouth, and his eyes did that lovely little ballet—looks me in the face, looks at my dick, looks up at me, closes his eyes as his mouth opens around the cockhead.

It was warm in there. He sucked lightly, flicking with his tongue. He wasn't ambitious.

I watched him for a second. "How you doing?"

"You in a hurry?" he blinked up at me, then closed his eyes again. He started sucking a little harder. I let myself down on one elbow, and he rose. His head started going up and down on my cock, just the right amount of pressure.

"That is nice," I cooed.

He smiled around my cock, then spit into his hand and wrapped it around me. "I can make it nicer."

"Go ahead."

He put his mouth back on me. It felt really good. It was quiet in the room, just our breathing and the traffic outside. I closed my eyes and concentrated on the sensations. "Mmm," I said.

He just kept doing it.

"Oh, man," I said. "Oh, that's good. Oh, baby. That's almost too good."

He slowed down a little. "I like to make it last," I said.

"Me, too."

I put my hand on his dick, still in his pants. "I'll tell you a story," I said. "I see you on a bus going cross country. When the bus stops at a diner for lunch, we end up in a booth together with a mother and a little girl. When we get back on the bus, I come and sit with you. When it gets dark, we touch each other's cocks, there on the bus. We make out and touch but that's all."

"Why is that all?"

"Because in my fantasy you're a straight boy."

"Hang on a minute." He got up suddenly, went to the bathroom, and came back sipping a glass of water. Getting back on the bed, he handed it to me to sip, then put it on the bedside table. "I like the feel of your cock," he said, and goes down on me some more.

"Do you want me to come?"

"You can. I can make you come."

"Yes, make me come."

He sucked, he tickled my balls, another hand snuck up to touch my nipple. He was a good cocksucker but it was his hand that was magic, rubbing my balls with the flat of his hand, then wrapping around the base of my prick, then doing a quick squeeze of the head.

"Mmm boy," I exulted. "Oh my. Yes, you're doing fine. Oh yes."

He went down on me so confidently. Looked up at me once in a while with a look that said he was enjoying. I hoped I could do as good a job on him.

"Oh yeah, yeah, yeah," I said. "Yes, do that."

I looked blindly at the beige walls of the motel room, the brass-colored metal frame around the obligatory picture, the dull blond wood headboard.

His fingertips were on my balls.

I got a fantasy of him kneeling in front of me, licking my balls while I jacked off, coming on his face, slapping him. This fantasy brought me closer. I urged him on, my voice rising. My eyes were squeezed shut now, all I saw was my mind's image of him kneeling in front of me, precome dribbling out of his cock as it stood up. That was the image that brought me to a climax, stuff leaking from his cock slit, kneeling for me and desiring me, being so turned on he gets wet.

I shoved upwards and he hung on. I was moaning, grunting, shooting in his mouth.

When I finished, we both sank back.

"Wow," I said after a second. It sounded a little obligatory to me, but I was in my just-came ecstasy and was serious.

He licked his lips, looked up at me like a porn star, the stuff in the corner of his mouth. I kissed him, sucking up some of my come.

We started kissing for real. I put my hands on his nipples again, doing my utmost to turn him on. I kissed him fast and carefully, trying to make him a little breathless. In passion we rolled around the bed. I worked his pants off and touched his cock with my fingertips. "I want this," I whispered.

"Yeah," he got out before I filled his mouth up with my tongue again.

I touched his cock slit. There was wetness coming out, as I had imagined. I spread the precome around his cockhead, then licked my fingers and got it wetter.

He lay on his back, resting his head on my shoulder. I looked down at his body. Stocky college kid, his belly ending in a dark vertical ridge of hair below the navel, leading down to his crotch.

I wanted to put my face right there, right at the base of his cock where he's hairiest. I wanted to smell him.

I jacked him off for a while, then went down on him. His cock fit in my mouth well. Like him it was not long, but thick. It made me feel full, blissful.

When I got into a rhythm, he said, "Mister, when you sat down next to me on the bus I was scared, but now I see you're just a big friendly fag, sucking my cock across the country. You make me feel good, friendly fag, you do. Come on, show a straight boy how it's done.

Is this what fags do with each other?"

"Mm-hmm."

"They suck each other's cocks like this. It's nasty. What other nasty things do they do? Just keep doing that—I'll tell you what they do. They put fingers in each other's asses. And they lick each other's assholes. And they fuck each other.... Is that right? Are you one of those men I was supposed to stay away from in the bus station?"

"Yep."

"And do faggots come in each other's mouths?"

"Yes." I sucked faster.

"Can I do that, even though I'm a straight boy and I've never done this?"

"Yes."

"Will it make me a faggot too?"

"Yes."

"I'll have to let other faggots come in my mouth."

"Yes."

He came, groaning, holding onto my hair. I sucked up his sperm and kept the pressure on his dick, made it more intense in the middle of his orgasm, then I grabbed his cock in my hand and hissed at him, "You're a faggot now, a cocksucker. Now you have to be one."

He moaned and bucked once more in my hand. I covered him with my mouth again as he sank back.

He caught his breath. "I liked that fantasy," he said.

"No way would I think you were a straight boy."

"On a bus, you wouldn't?"

"On a bus I'd pick you out right away. We'd be seat mates long before we got to the first lunch stop. But you're right. That idea of perverting a straight boy—such a turn-on. Makes me want to join a fraternity."

"Oh, stop," he cried in mock horror, covering his face.

"Uh-oh, too close to home."

He lowered his hands and we smiled at each other.

"So, what do we do now?" I asked.

"Do you want to meet my Daddy?"

⌒

We drove in his car up the hill into Pacific Heights, and circled to find a parking space. Cary told me he was living with a middle-aged guy who was a rich businessman. The guy had just started to invest in male porn flicks. "Mainly he just sends ten-thousand-dollar checks to his partner in North Hollywood and when he's down there, visits the set in the hope he'll get to suck off some nineteen-year-old stud."

"Pretty expensive blowjob," I said.

"Well, at least he's not giving it to the Republicans."

We walked a couple of blocks on Vallejo Street and turned up a brick stairway in front of a huge Victorian house. "It's a flat here," Cary said.

He let us in and we climbed another set of stairs up to the landing. I could hear a television playing. "Hey," he called.

We went into a living room, decorated expensively if anonymously in postmodern Italian. There was a huge couch upholstered in bone-colored fabric. On one end sat a fiftyish man, his hair closely cropped like Cary's, staring at the television. On the tube, contestants on a reality show were running some kind of race on a sand dune.

"Look what I brought home," Cary said. "Jim, this is Sam. Sam, Jim."

Jim leapt up with his hand out. As we shook hands, Cary went over to him and kissed him and cuddled in the arm thrown over his shoulder—Jim was nearly a head taller. Looking at me from that shelter, Cary said to him, "We tricked down on Lombard Street."

The man smiled at me. "Get you something?"

"Got any gin?"

"Cary, make some martinis. Okay?"

"Sure," I answered.

"Have a seat over here." He went over to the couch. "I'm rooting for the old guy," he said, nodding toward the televised race. "He's a fireman turned lawyer. Courage combined with ruthlessness."

"Are all lawyers ruthless?"

"I'm in insurance; I should know." He picked up the remote and turned the TV off.

Cary brought the drinks. We made small talk and in half an hour were suitably buzzed.

"Now that we're uninhibited," Jim said, "whattaya say we get down to business?"

"Okay, but I have all the insurance I need."

"That's not the kind of business I was thinking of. I was thinking of this." And he stood up and opened up his pants and took out his cock. It was big.

"I see."

"I hope you do. Here's your chance to back out."

"What do you think I came over for?"

"You tell me. What do you want to do? Watch Boy suck my cock? He's awful pretty when he does that. On the other hand, I'd kind of like to see him suck your cock too."

Cary came over and sat on the arm of the sofa and started playing with my nipples through my shirt. "Both of those are kind of nice," I said, meaning his suggestions.

"Or do you want to fuck his mouth while I fuck him with this? I've found it's a good way to keep him in line. Or we can do some nasty stuff too. But maybe that's a little heavy on the first date."

The kid was turning me on, the way he was touching me. "You could still tell me about it even if we don't do it."

"Boy sits on my face and I lick his asshole while he sticks needles into my tits. If you wanted to, you could sit on my cock and make out with him while he did that."

"This is turning me on."

"Why don't you show me how it turns you on?"

I kicked off my shoes and dropped my pants. With my right hand I took hold of my cock and started stroking myself. "Keep talking," I said.

"We could put you in the sling. See those bolts?" He motioned to the bar area, where there were some posts with big eye bolts. "It goes up in about one minute. I'd stand and fuck you with my cock, while Boy stands behind your head. You bend your head back and suck his balls while you get fucked, and he'd give you poppers to sniff and you'd be in fucking outer space."

"Yeah."

"Any of that appeal to you?"

"Let's start from the top," I said, letting go of my cock for a second. "I don't know how much of that I can do tonight. But it turns me on to hear about it."

"Great. Boy, get over here and suck me. Sam, if you jack off while he sucks me, I'll talk dirty for you. How's that."

"Great."

"Just don't come right away. We got plenty of time, if you do. Come over and sit on this ottoman and face me. Little Boy can kneel between us."

He kicked an upholstered ottoman a few feet away from the armchair and got rid of his clothes except for a tank top undershirt. From under the cushion of the armchair he produced a couple of trick towels. He spread one on the armchair and handed the other to me. We both plopped down, me still with my pants around my ankles.

"Go ahead, take those off. I don't want you running out of here."

"I'm not planning on leaving that quickly." I kicked them off.

Daddy—that's how I was thinking of him, and that's who he looked like in that wife-beater—declined to lay back on the armchair's cushions. He sat upright on the edge of the chair, as Cary slipped in between us. Daddy produced a plastic bottle of lube from the same place as the towels and handed it to me.

Cary, who had stripped naked, knelt down and put his face in Daddy's crotch. I made sure Daddy could see me behind his head.

"Yeah, show me what my boy ate," he said, leering at me as I began stroking my dick. "Did you fuck him or did he just suck you?"

"We blew each other."

"Yeah, he's a cocksucking slut, aren't you, boy?"

Cary already had his mouth full. "Mm-hmm," he affirmed.

"Just make sure you fuck him in front of me," Daddy went on. "I love to see him get fucked."

"Uh-huh," I said. "Why do you like to see your boy get fucked?"

"It's beautiful. I'll let you watch too. I don't want to spoil it. Keep jacking off your cock."

"I am. It feels good."

"It looks good. Keep doing it. And you," he said, laying a heavy hand on Cary's head, "keep sucking, boy. Suck it like a good boy. Earn your keep."

"Yes, Daddy," Cary paused long enough to say.

"Are you going to come in his mouth?" I asked.

He just smiled at me. I didn't think he was going to come because he probably had just one in him, but since Cary and I had already come that night, we were probably only good for one each as well. Maybe it would turn out to be a short evening.

That's when he brought out the poppers. He sure had a lot of stuff crammed somewhere under the cushions of his armchair.

He passed the vial in front of his face and took a shallow breath, then let out a groan. Cary made a noise too, so I knew it had had an effect on Daddy's cock, or maybe Daddy just thrust deeper. I decided I wanted to see more of what was happening so I slid off the ottoman and knelt next to Cary on the floor. I could see his face as he went up and down on the prick.

"Hey cocksucker, hey fag," I said. "Look at the little cocksucker getting himself fucked in the mouth. It's the way I said: Once a faggot does it once, he has to do it for everybody. Look at you doing that. Look at your mouth crammed full of dick." He made no sign of having heard me; he had his eyes closed and was concentrating on the oral universe.

"Want some?" asked Daddy, offering me the poppers.

"A little." I sniffed the foul odor and immediately felt a wave of dizziness mixed with intense physical sensation. My cock seemed to double in size, although I knew that was just because it was doubly sensitive. "Fuck," I whined, my heart pounding.

"Oh yeah," Daddy said approvingly, noting I had started to jack myself off harder.

The poppers made me lose a chunk of inhibitions. I climbed up on the armchair, my feet on either side of Daddy's thighs, and pushed my balls in his face. He licked them obligingly and tried to suck them into his mouth, but I don't like that. "You want something in your mouth?" I asked, aiming my cock downward.

He slammed his head forward on it, making me feel his throat. That's the thing with these older guys, they have sucked so many cocks in their lives that their gag reflexes are practically nonexistent. They'd suffocate before they gagged. That doesn't mean their throats aren't muscled and tight. "Woo boy," I said.

Daddy was making growling noises in his throat. I looked down and saw him dragging his fingernails up his legs over and over, making long white scratches. I was still holding the poppers in my left hand and gave him another whiff. His throat spasmed and my cock sank a little deeper. After a few seconds his face started to get red and I pulled out a little. He took a big breath then, so I must have been too deep, all right.

I started thrusting in and out, trying to get a little closer to coming without actually doing it. Daddy was still scratching the hell out of his legs and making growling noises. I gave him another hit of the poppers every once in a while. I was grateful he was getting into it so much; my cock was no bigger than Cary's, so I knew it couldn't have been anything special about me.

I decided I wanted to suck Daddy's cock too, and got down from the armchair and sat down on the floor next to Cary. He seemed deep in a trance, his eyes squeezed shut and his mouth plugged up. I watched his ass move back and forth slightly with his movements, and debated whether to touch him there. There was something so intense about his concentration that I didn't want to disturb it. But after a while he sensed my presence next to him and brought himself back from wherever he was. He slowed his movements, took a deep breath around Daddy's cock, and reached out for my hand, although he kept his eyes closed. His hand was cold and I warmed it in both my hands as he continued to lick and rub his face against Daddy's dick.

"I have to take a shit," Daddy announced loudly. "Then I want to get fucked."

He stood up abruptly, brushing Cary aside, and stomped off down the hall. Cary rolled onto the floor on his back, but he still kept hold of my hand.

I lay down next to Cary—we were on an oriental rug that covered a rectangle of floor space in front of the living room furniture—and kissed him. He kissed me back for a minute, then said, "I need to rest a second."

"Okay sure," I said. I reached down and cupped his balls. His cock, half hard, stirred gently against my hand. I rubbed the heel of my thumb against the underside of his penis and tickled his balls with my fingertips. It made me want to put my mouth there, so I scooched down and nuzzled him.

He sighed and put his hand on the back of my head. "Stick around a little," he said. "It's good to have someone else here."

Before I could answer that, the doorbell rang. I jumped a little, and we both sat up.

"Aw fuck," he said, "who could that be?"

"Get the door!" yelled Daddy from someplace deep within the house.

"Yeah okay!" He stood up, went into the hallway, and clicked on an intercom. "Who is it?!"

A squawking sound came from the speaker.

"What do you want?" Cary answered. More squawking. "Aw, shit!" he replied.

"Who the fuck is it?" Daddy called.

"It's Dirk and some of his whore friends."

"Great! The more the merrier!" The sound of flushing.

"Aw Jim!"

"Don't 'aw Jim' me, boy," Daddy said, coming out into the hall, still pulling up his pants. He went over to the speaker and hit a button. "You're gonna mess up—what's his name again?" He jerked a thumb in my direction.

"Sam."

"You're gonna mess up Sam's chance to meet a star."

"Fuck," Cary said, stomping away, leaving Daddy in the hall. I was still on the floor, wearing nothing but a T-shirt, so I got uncertainly to my feet and reached for my clothes. I only got the briefs on when three guys came up the stairs.

"There's my big daddy!" cried the one in the lead. I had my pants in my hand and was standing on one leg, but I froze there as I recognized Dirk Powers, one of that year's most famous gay porn stars. Six-foot-five, arms thickly muscled, his skin the color of a basketball, he air-kissed Jim and swept into the room. His "whore friends," who were no less handsome in the same porn-star way, followed.

"Look, a flamingo," one of them said cheerfully.

I put my leg through my pants. "Hello," I said.

"Did we interrupt something?" Dirk brayed. "Jim, you slut, isn't your chino houseboy enough for you?"

"This is Sam," Jim said. "Sam, meet Dirk Powers."

We shook hands. I still had only one leg in my pants so I held the trousers up with my left. "Glad to meet you," I said.

"Mmm," Dirk said, glancing at me briefly. "Jimmy boy! I've come for some honey!"

"Christ, Dirk, I told you, nothing until the distributor gets the tapes back from the dupe house."

Dirk's buddies went back into the hallway and slouched against the banister as Dirk went up to Jim and stood very close. "Now, Daddy, is that any way to treat your little porn star?" He gazed into Jim's eyes and planted a hand on his chest. Pushing his crotch forward, he cooed quietly at Jim, who blushed. "Hmm? Hmm? Is it?" he repeated.

"You slut," Jim said quietly. "You think you can just come in here and hit me up for cash?"

"Yeah, Daddy, that is what I think. I'm just like a college girl who comes home from freshman year all knocked up and needs money to fix a little problem."

"Oh, you need a fix, is that it?"

Dirk pouted. "Nothing like that. Just something to take these tired whores out on the town with."

"Speak for yourself, bitch," one of them retorted.

"Please, Daddy?" Dirk reached between Jim's legs and laughed, "Oh, my, you *were* occupied!"

Jim snorted and pushed the younger man away. "Come on," he said.

"You're just my big sugar daddy," the performer said gaily.

They retreated down the hallway and disappeared into the back of the house. Left alone with Dirk's companions, I finished putting on my clothes. I stood there for a second and then sat down on the couch. We regarded each other. Finally one of them spoke up. "Hey," he said, "are you Jim's boy?"

"No, I'm just visiting," I said.

"I'm Ron. This is Justin. We came up from L.A. with Dirk."

"Sam."

"Do you want to come and party with us?" He was wearing a light blue tank top and nothing else. I thought maybe he was on Ecstasy or something to be that warm.

"I don't know, where are you going?" I said.

"Polk Street." He came over and sat next to me, throwing his arm over my shoulders. I took a look at his eyes and they did a little jiggity-jig—certainly he was on some kind of speed.

He put his hand on my crotch. I didn't push it away but I didn't feel like opening my pants yet again either. "I think I've had all the partying I need for tonight. Maybe you can give me a ride back to my car."

"Sure, whatever." He rested his head on my shoulder and pressed lightly on my crotch. I realized I was a little tense because I didn't want Cary to come out and see us like this; I wanted Cary to come out and come home with me.

We sat there for a while and then, after a long time, Dirk emerged from the back of the house, followed by Jim. "We can go to Basix and drink margaritas," Dirk was saying. "It's the perfect time of year to come, it's hot."

"Yeah, sure," Jim was saying. Cary was nowhere in sight.

Ron bounced to his feet and joined Dirk and the other fellow. Without another word, Dirk led the way down the stairs and his companions followed.

I looked at Jim. "These guys are giving me a ride back to my car," I said, embarrassed.

"Mm-hmm," he said.

"See ya," I said.

He looked at me uncomfortably and mumbled, "Um, yeah."

Downstairs there was a limo double-parked. We piled into the back, where there was a sort of U-shaped seat, like a corner booth at Denny's. Ron and I sat at the ends of the U, facing each other. He looked at me insouciantly and then jerked his chin at my crotch. "Let's see it," he said. The others laughed.

I stared back for a minute and then opened my trousers and took it out, sticky from the lube. Ron sprang out of his seat and scooped my cock into his mouth as the car started moving.

"Suck it, my pretty!" leered Dirk.

"The party's started for Ron," Justin remarked. "We're starting the clock; come on, boy."

Ron started in on me. My dick stiffened in his mouth and he reached blindly over to Justin, who was sitting next to me. Laughing, Justin opened his pants and placed his cock in Ron's hand. The driver had put on some cheesy house music, so the scene was now exactly like a porn movie with the soundtrack thumping away.

"My, my, my," cheered Dirk. "Where's the camera? This is good."

"I actually just need a ride to my car," I said, my voice unsteady.

"Where is it?" Dirk laughed. I told him and he relayed the information to the driver, who completely ignored the goings-on. Probably what happened every night in his limo.

Ron was doing good work. I was embarrassed and turned on and tense and excited. I had half a mind to go with these fags and take Ecstasy and dance all night. Ron sucked me obsessively, the E making my cock feel good in his mouth. I knew if he kept doing that I was going to come.

As the car turned right, I was pressed backward into my side-facing seat. Ron went deep on my cock and touched my balls and started sucking and jacking me off. He had his other hand on Justin's prick and I was staring at it. It was huge, of course, because they were all porn actors; maybe I'd seen the prick before in videos, ramming into Dirk's or somebody else's asshole. I was staring at the giant fat cock being jerked off and feeling this other guy's mouth on my prick and being rocked this way and that by the motion of the car. At one moment I was thrown in Justin's direction, almost close enough to touch his cock with my lips, then thrown in the other direction away from it.

"Yeah baby," Dirk sneered in his best porn-star tough-guy voice. "You fuck him. You fuck his fat whore mouth. Come in it, baby. Oh, yeah, baby. Oh, yeah." And the music went *thumpa-thumpa-thumpa-thumpa, d-d-d-d-d-d-d-duh!*

I closed my eyes, listening to the voice and the insistent music, feeling the delicious sensations in my prick. Except for the motion of the car, I could have been at a peep show down on Folsom Street. I could feel an orgasm gathering in my balls like a tiny, angry storm. Behind us on the hill, Cary and his daddy were settling in for a long night.

Incest

1

On the last day of school, you don't do anything. You've gotten all your papers back, all the tests are done, and all the kids sit sideways in their seats talking while the teacher sits up front and reads a book. Everyone gossips about the sixth and seventh grade prom the week before, and the party afterward that turned into a big makeout session for some people—who made out with whom, who let the boys touch them, who had to call their parents at 1 A.M. after waking up in the den with their clothing all messed up. A lot of what we talked about never happened, but that never stops us.

Each class was like that. There was a special class schedule, where we went to all classes, even though on a normal week the classes were staggered so we would only go to five out of our seven classes on a normal day. We went to each class in order, for forty minutes, with no lunch. It was like a marathon tour of everybody I loved and hated, everybody who made me sick, everybody who snubbed me, everybody who I wrote notes with and paged all year long. It's so weird to be sitting in fifth period and it's only 11:30 in the morning; usually it's after lunch.

So there's a weird feeling to the day, time is all out of whack, and the whole year is running before your eyes like you're dying. But you're not dying; seventh grade is dying.

All during fifth period I waited for my pager to go off. I knew Jenna Sondstrom was going to page me, because she had Office Assistance during fifth period and always managed to dial a few people even though she wasn't supposed to. On a day like today, I figured, she's probably dialing Japan, she's dialing the moon. Today you could get away with anything.

Sure enough, halfway through the forty minutes my pager vibrated and I jumped, which made all my friends crack up. I mean, they weren't really my friends, they were just the people I talked to in that class.

Switching the pager off, I yanked it from my belt to read:

28-6-55-143-10

Which in code means:

See you (or C U, which you get by pressing 2 and 8 on the phone)
6th period (6)
Something special to tell you (55, which looks just like SS)
I love you (which have 1, 4, and 3 letters respectively)
Jenna (J, which is the 10th letter, her usual signature)

"What's it say?" "Who's it from?" "Let me see!" shouted the other girls.

"Girls, quiet down," said the teacher from the front, not even looking up from his book.

I'd already nuked the message. Actually Jenna had sent me just about the same message every day, except for the SS part. And half the time she would say she had something special to tell me, but it would just be more gossip.

I didn't care, because I love getting pages from Jenna, my best friend and then some.

"It's from Jeff," suggested Mariah, a half-black, half-Mexican girl with frizzy black hair.

"Jeff loves her," said Kylie, another Mexican girl.

"He danced with you at the prom," said Harmony, a white girl with cool straight hair and bruises.

They thought ten meant Jeff. Nobody knew it was Jenna, which was weird because she'd been paging me every day.

"Shut up, you guys," I smiled at them, which only confirmed their suspicions. "Jeff! Jeff!" they yelled. If they wanted to think it's Jeff, that was okay with me. He was in third period and I didn't have to see him ever again, or until August.

"Jeff is bad," I said mysteriously, and they practically screamed with delight. As I planned, this got the teacher to tell us all to shut up, which meant I didn't have to explain anything.

In sixth period I met Jenna outside the door as usual. She smiled as she came up to me, which made me tingle. I am so in love with Jenna.

She gave me a pen she stole from the office and I handed her a note I wrote in fourth period and we went inside the classroom.

This class was taught by mean Mrs. Tanner, who not only didn't let us sit where we wanted, even though it was the last day of the year, but actually expected to get something done. We sat in our assigned seats, with Jenna one seat in front and one row over.

Mrs. Tanner read us a news story about the election, which was so lame. We can't even vote until we're eighteen, so who cares? I spent the whole period looking at Jenna, who thoughtfully turned slightly in her seat so I could see her profile, and the whole period long I drew pictures of her in my notebook with the pen she stole for me. My notebook was about two-thirds drawings, starting from the back, and one-fifth class notes, starting from the front. That left a lot of blank pages.

Jenna had not told me the something special, and the anticipation, combined with the last-day-of-school bursting feeling, made me feel like screaming. But Mrs. Tanner was so mean that everybody just sat and scowled, and when she started asking questions about the article, the kiss-ass kids answered like always.

Finally we got out. There was only one more period left in seventh grade. The minute the bell rang, I jumped into the aisle and crouched down next to her seat. "What is it?" I asked. "What did you want to tell me?"

She bit her lower lip, the way she always did when she had something great to say. I loved it when she did that.

"My parents say I can have a slumber party on my birthday."

"But that's not till July! That's, like, two months from now. Can't you have one before then?"

"No, it's a reward for being good all summer."

"But that's hella long!"

"It's okay, we can take between now and then to plan it."

"Oh yeah! Okay!"

She got up and we walked into the hallway together, down toward the T where she goes left, I go right, for seventh period.

"Come on over tomorrow," she said.

"Okay."

Seventh period passed in a blur. The pent-up energy of the kids was so great that it was like we were playing dodge ball with no ball. I sat in my seat with the familiar tingle I always got from seeing Jenna. 143-10, 143-10, I repeated to myself over and over. I wanted to write a song with that as the chorus.

When the last bell rang, everybody tumbled out of the building like it was on fire. In fact we never moved that fast for a fire drill.

I went out to the special pickup area. Kids who get picked up by parents and stuff go to a turnaround where cars can pull up. Teachers supervised and checked the ID of everybody who picked us up, on account of a kidnapping that happened that year. When I saw my sister's old Ford Fairlane, a weird older car that looks like it should be in a museum, I bounced forward. She showed her badge to the gym teacher who was supervising, and I got in.

"How's it going, Julie?" asked the gym teacher, this weird guy who always acted creepy with her.

"Hey there, Frank. It's going good," she said. She turned away from him, winked at me, and drove off.

"He's such a sociopath," I said, encouraged by the wink.

"He's not a sociopath," she said. "He's just a guy on the make. A sociopath is somebody like the guy in that movie we rented last weekend."

"I thought that was a psychopath."

"Sometimes it's hard to know the difference."

"Hey, Jenna is having a slumber party in July."

"All right. How was the last day of school?"

"Excruciating." She laughed. She always thought it was funny when I used big words, so I use them as much as possible.

Julie, who was twenty, took care of me and my brother, who was sixteen. Since our parents died four years ago, supposedly we belonged to our aunt and uncle who lived in town then, but then they got divorced and even though Aunt Donna moved only a few miles away, Julie was doing most of the taking-care the whole time. She loved us, even if she was mean sometimes. She worked at night, so she always picked me up from school.

We went into the house and I flopped down on the bed. The tingling feeling wasn't stopping—in fact, it seemed to be getting stronger. I didn't know what I was feeling.

I started reading, to wait for dinnertime. Then I felt it—like there was something wet in me. That was weird.

I went to the bathroom to look. From out of my slit, which had hardly any hair around it, a little trickle of blood was running.

I put a finger in it and felt it, warm. It was a little scary, I admit, but more because it was exciting.

"Julie," I called. "You'd better come see."

She came to the bathroom. I already had the door cracked open and she opened it the rest of the way. She was petite, an inch taller than me, with the same long brown hair. Hers was cut shorter, above her shoulders; mine reached down between my shoulder blades. "I'm kind of busy, Kelly," she said.

"It's kind of important." I scooped a finger between my legs and held it up for her to see. "Blood."

"Let me see." She came over and took my hand in hers and looked at my finger. She looked at it for a long time.

I wasn't sure what she was thinking about. It felt like I was waiting for a decision or a verdict of some kind, as if I had confessed something bad to a teacher and was standing silently in front of her desk waiting for her to decide whether to punish me. Julie was good to us, although, as I said, sometimes she could be not nice. I wasn't sure she was going to be nice.

Then Julie bent her head forward and licked my bloody finger. "Hmm," she said. "I think so. But I have to make sure."

Before I knew it, she had dipped a finger between my pussy lips and scooped up a little of the blood on her own finger. The touch sent shock waves through me. I didn't know what to think. Was this nice or not?

She lifted her own finger, now with my blood on it, to her lips and put it in her mouth. "Yes, I think so," she said.

"So what do I do now?" I asked.

She had her eyes closed for a moment. Then she opened them and smiled down at me. "Well, you can't spend four days a month sitting on the toilet, so you need to learn how to handle it." So she quickly explained about Tampax and tampons and all that other girl stuff, and when she was finished with the explanation, she said, "I'll show you."

She started unbuttoning her jeans. We still take baths together once in a while, so this wasn't a big deal.

"Up till now, I've taught you it's not really nice to look at somebody who's naked," she said, pulling the jeans down over her hips and kicking them off. Then she removed her panties, white ones with little red and yellow flowers. "But obviously you have to look now because I'm showing you."

"Okay." I didn't mention that I'd stolen lots of glances before, when she would take me to the pool and we changed in the locker room, or sometimes very early in the morning when she would stumble naked to the bathroom. I had looked at her naked at those times because I had wanted to see what I would look like when I grew up. So I'll tell you that my sister had a lot of hair between her legs, hair that grew up to a point halfway to her belly button. I had almost none, and I was always half excited, and half frightened, to see how much I would have some day. I didn't know it back then, when I was stealing glances at my sister's pussy, but I know now that compared to other women we are really hairy. Sometimes other people even find it startling. But I grew up thinking it was normal.

But when I was twelve, like I said, I had hardly any.

She took a tampon out of its paper wrapper. Then she took a little plastic bottle out of the medicine cabinet. It was filled with a clear fluid. "This is the lube I use sometimes when I have to stick something up my cunt or my ass," she said. "It's really made for sex, but you can use it for anything that has to go up there. You usually don't use it for a tampon, because your cunt is already somewhat wet from the blood. But I have to use it today to show you, because I'm not on my period."

I watched her put a little lube on her hand and smear it on her cunt. "I have to get some inside too," she said, and pushed some inside with her fingers. When she added another finger to the one that was already inside, I saw her lick her lips.

It gave me a strange feeling. On the one hand, I thought that what she was doing was not nice, exactly. On the other hand, it made me tingle between my legs. I had only felt that way around Jenna, so I wasn't sure what it meant if I felt like that while watching my sister put fingers in her cunt.

"Okay. So what you do is this: Just push it up inside you. Go real slow because it's not a straight shot—you've got things that get in the way a little. So just go real slow and feel it. There." The tampon was inside her, a little string hanging out.

"What's that, the rip cord?" I joked.

"Yeah, well seriously, sometimes you can accidentally sort of suck it up inside you. The string helps you keep track of it."

"Okay."

"Now you try. You might want to stand up and put one foot up on the toilet. I'll help."

Crouching down on floor in front of me, she tore open another tampon. I stood up, one foot up and my knees wide open, my cunt at her eye level. There was a tiny dribble of blood coming out. She looked at it avidly.

Handing me the tampon, she said, "Let me just see if you need any lube." She touched my cunt gently.

I pulled up on my mound to see better. She touched my cunt lips and then dipped her finger in the stream of blood and spread it around the lips. "I just want to make sure you're a little wet all around." I closed my eyes and felt her touch me. When I opened my eyes I saw my nipples had gotten hard. My breasts started that year, and they were already pretty big—at least they felt pretty big to me. Of course they were not as big as hers.

"I'll just put a finger a little ways inside. Just to make sure you're wet enough." She started easing her finger in—just her finger-tip—and sort of squiggled it around a little.

This also felt strange, in the way that watching her touch her-self felt strange: scary and exciting at the same time. Actually, I was used to her touching me, because we would wash each other when we take baths. But she had never done anything like that before. Nobody had. *Wicked* was the word that suddenly came to mind.

She put her finger in a little farther. "How does that feel?" she asked intently. "It doesn't hurt, does it?"

"No," I answered. How did it feel? It felt wicked. It was like that Jenna-type feeling. I realized I could feel my heart beating. My mouth was dry and I couldn't take my eyes off my cunt. The sight of her finger there was fascinating.

She kept pressing her finger in just a little and then wiggling it around. "I'm moving it around to make sure it's wet all over," she said. "As long as it's wet, it won't hurt."

"It feels pretty wet," I said. My voice was shaking a little. I was watching. I wanted her to keep doing it.

She put the finger in even farther. It was almost all the way in. I started breathing through my mouth. "I think you'll be okay," she said, taking the finger out, smeared with blood. When she took it all the way out, I gasped.

"God," I said.

"Did that feel good to you?" she asked lightly. "That's one way people masturbate, you know."

"Oh, yeah?"

"We talked about that, right? It's what you do to feel good down there. Have you done it?"

"Well, I don't know. Not like that."

"Well, you can," she said. She ran some water in the sink and washed off her finger.

I positioned my own finger in front of my cunt and prepared to put it in, but I hesitated. I had the feeling she hadn't meant I could do it right then. But I wanted to; or actually I wanted her to do it again, but she was already handing me the fresh tampon.

"Now, before you put it in, let me wash you a little."

I stood passively, one foot on the toilet, the tampon in my hand, as she turned back to the sink. She ran warm water over a washcloth while I stood there.

"Do you do it like that?" I asked.

"Sometimes," she said with a half smile.

"You want me to stay like this?" I asked.

"No, sit down on the toilet," she said. She suddenly sounded a little mad; her face was serious. I sat down. "Spread your legs," she said tightly. I didn't know what had happened to change her mood, and I hoped I hadn't done anything wrong.

She knelt between my knees and reached in. I felt the wet warmth of the washcloth hit me, and I found myself involuntarily pushing forward against it.

"I can't see if you do that," she said. "Lean back. Just relax."

She ran the washcloth gently up and down on my pussy while I looked at her face. Then she looked up at me. "I'll bet this feels good, too," she said.

"It does," I said. "It makes me sort of want to pee, too."

"Oh, okay. Well, you can do that, and I'll wash you again." She withdrew her hand and sat back on her heels, still looking between my legs.

"Are you going to stay there?" I asked. I wanted to know if she was going to keep looking at my cunt like that. It was a little embarrassing, but I also wanted her to keep doing it. It was doing something to me.

"Yes, I want to see if it's all right. Sometimes when you're on your period the flow of your pee is a little different."

"Different how?"

"Just different. Go ahead."

I tried. I'd had to go a minute before, and now it was a little difficult. "I don't know if I can do it with you looking."

"Oh, well, okay. Let's try it with the washcloth." She ran more warm water on the washcloth and knelt down and pressed it between my legs again. "Don't be shy," she said. The warmth was back in her voice. "It's just me."

The heat from the washcloth did the trick. Pee started coming out of me. "Oh, I'm doing it," I said.

"I can tell. Just keep going."

She held the washcloth against my pussy for a moment longer, then relaxed so that it wasn't pressing, just resting against me. She leaned back a little. I looked down but I couldn't really see anything. Then I closed my eyes. I heard her take a deep breath. My piss continued to run out.

"That's right," she said. "Just piss. That's right. Now I'm going to take the washcloth away and look at it coming out. Is that okay? I can see it fine."

"What?" I asked, my voice barely audible.

"I can see you piss."

"Uh-huh?"

I could hear it ping against the toilet bowl, and I could hear her breathing.

Finally I finished. She rinsed out the washcloth again. "Looked okay to me," she said. There was a funny quiver in her voice—not the stern tone that she had used a moment before, but a sort of nervousness, sort of like the way I was feeling.

She ran the washcloth between my legs one more time and then tossed it into the sink. "When you wash off your cunt before putting in a tampon, make sure you don't wash inside. You don't want to wipe away any of the moisture. Just the outside."

"Okay."

"Now stand up and try putting it in. Put your foot up."

It went in pretty easily. There must have been a lot of moisture.

"Leave the string hanging out. That's right," she said. As she stood up and went to wash her hands, she said, "Now, you change it when it gets too soaked and blood starts to come out again, or, if it doesn't get too soaked you have to take it out in six or eight hours. Don't leave it in longer than that."

"Okay." I took my foot off the toilet.

She hugged me, both of us wearing nothing but a T-shirt. "I'm really happy for you, honey," she said. "I've been looking forward to this day your whole life."

As she turned away, I took one more look at her pussy.

I went back and tried to get on with my reading, but it was impossible for me to keep out of my mind what had just happened. I went to have a glass of water while she went out to the garden.

I drank a big glass of iced tea from the fridge and tried to read, but my mind kept wandering. I was thinking about what if felt like to have Julie press that washcloth between my legs and tell me to pee. The more I thought about it, the more I felt like doing it again. But unless I played dumb and asked for her to "show" me again, I doubted it would happen.

I finished the glass of tea and went and got another. If I couldn't pee while she was watching, at least I could do it myself. I sat there and drank and tried to read, but really I was just waiting for my bladder to fill.

Finally I had to pee again and I went into the bathroom. I sat down on the toilet, but before I started, I jumped up and got the wash-cloth where it was hanging on the towel rack. I ran hot water over it, and then sat down on the toilet and pressed it between my legs the way she had. It felt good, and when I started peeing, I rubbed myself gently.

I found that the more I rubbed, the better it felt. Finally I stopped peeing, but I sat there a while longer.

After a second I tossed the washcloth into the sink and reached down between my legs. I pressed the flat of my fingers against my cunt, and it felt good a little, but not as good as the washcloth, and not nearly as good as when she did it. I decided I would have to figure out a way for her to do it again.

We had dinner—me, Julie, and Jason, our brother. For dinner he came out of his room, where he spends as many waking hours as he can, playing games on the internet with people, messaging his friends, probably looking at dirty pictures for all I know. He sat and rubbed his eyes as he ate. His high school had let out the week before, and I don't think he'd been in the sunlight since.

"What's new, Jason?" asked Julie, watching him inhale macaroni and cheese.

"Uhn, nothin'," he muttered.

"Kelly's last day of seventh grade was today," Julie announced.

"Nice goin', kid."

"Now I'm an eighth grader."

"Eighth grade sucked," Jason announced.

"Is Jason a sociopath?" I asked Julie.

"He's getting there."

"Shut up, you guys."

After dinner he disappeared into his bedroom again.

I spent the evening reading—for some reason, it seemed like the thing to do, rather than watching TV or talking on the phone. I couldn't get my mind off what was happening down there inside me, especially because I had what felt like a sock stuffed into my crack. I counted the hours and minutes until it was time to check it again.

Finally, after the tampon had been in exactly six hours, I went to her and said excitedly, "Julie, can you come in the bathroom again, please?"

"Sure," she said casually. She got up from the desk where she had been working and followed me down the hallway. We went into the bathroom and shut the door.

I stood over by the toilet. "My tampon's been in for six hours now."

"Do you want to take it out?"

"Uh-huh."

"Okay; well, do what you did before. Put your leg up on the toilet and take it out."

"I thought I might have to put some of that stuff on my pussy first."

"Oh, really?" she said. I saw her purse her lips. "You don't really have to."

"I want to. It feels better."

"Okay, here. You don't have to ask permission to use it." She handed me the little bottle and leaned back casually on the sink.

"Maybe you'd better put it on."

She looked at me. "Is that what you want?"

"Yeah." Please do it, I thought. Please say yes.

"Okay. Take your pants off."

She stood there watching me while I took my pants and panties off. I handed her the lube.

She put some lube onto her fingertips and gently touched my pussy. I jumped a little. "Is it cold?" she smiled. "Sorry."

She spread it around my pussy lips. I closed my eyes and felt it. When she stopped, I opened my eyes and saw her looking back at me.

We stood there in silence a little. Finally I said, "Just a little more."

"Just a little more what?" she asked.

"Just a little more lube."

"Where?"

"On my pussy."

"Okay." She put it on her hand again and spread it on my cunt. She did it a little harder this time. I guess I pressed back a little, but she didn't stop. "You have to tell me what you want. I can't guess."

"Oh, really?" I said. I don't think I was thinking straight. I was breathing through my mouth by this time. I realized I was pressing back against her hand. I didn't know if that was all right, and I suddenly wanted to do it really hard. But I didn't dare move too much because it might be the wrong thing to do, and I didn't want her to stop.

"Does that feel good?"

"Yes."

"Tell me when it feels good."

"It feels good."

"Remember, you have to tell me."

She did it for a little while longer. I felt my face flushing. She stopped. "That's enough." She rinsed her hand off in the sink. "That's probably something you should do for yourself, you know."

"I like it when you do it."

"Really." I wasn't sure what that meant—do you really, or yeah you really like it.

She turned to face me. "Go ahead," she nodded. I began rubbing my pussy the way she had.

"I didn't mean that," she said. Now she was blushing. "I meant, go ahead and take out your tampon."

I took it out gently. It came out, soaked in blood. She told me to wrap it in toilet paper and throw it away, and to put another in.

She watched me put it in. She watched me the whole time.

We did that for the next couple of days. By the next time I

didn't even have to ask her to come with me. I just had to go up to her and say, "Ahem." Then she would go with me and shut the bathroom door behind us and help me.

I think back on those few days now with such longing. All I thought about for three days was the last time we were together and the next time we would do it. In between times, while I was waiting for the six hours to be up, I would drink water, gatorade, juice, iced tea, anything—gallons of it—so that I would have to pee. Then I would wait until I was bursting. Finally I would go into the bathroom and sit down with my warm washcloth and pee into it. Once I put my hand into the stream of piss and cupped it and let it run over into the toilet. The piss would be clear because I was drinking so much water, but it was still warm. I brought my hand closer to my pussy until I was touching my cunt while I peed. That made the pee go all over, so I took my hand out.

I wanted to pee and pee. Once when I heard Julie in the bathroom, I thought about going in there to watch her do it—if she could watch me, why couldn't I watch her? I didn't have the nerve, but I promised myself I would figure out a way.

On the fourth day, the tampon came out with hardly any blood on it at all. Looking at it with an amused expression, she said, "I guess you're done."

"Julie," I said.

"Yes, sweetheart?"

"Do we have to stop?"

"Stop what?"

"You know."

"You'd better tell me," she said, leaning in that casual way against the sink. "Stop what?"

I sat on the toilet and opened my legs. "You know," I said. "When you touch me. And when you look at me. When you hold your hand against me and I pee all over it and you look at me. It feels good. I don't want to stop."

She looked at me sitting on the toilet.

"Well, you said you wanted me to tell you."

"Ahem," she said. "I guess I did. That's a good girl—you always tell me the truth when I ask you."

I realized I was blushing all over with the wicked feeling. I felt embarrassed but, at the same time, in a way proud. Like telling her that and getting her approval had been the right thing to do. Not just in an approval way but in a confession way. Like that feeling of standing in front of the teacher, only you're positive this time that she's not going to punish you, but that she just wants you to tell her what you did, for your own good.

Then she said, "You know, it's all right. I mean, it's not wrong to do it. But you're still a little young to be doing this, you know?"

"What do you mean? I've got my period. I can't help it."

"That's not what I meant. It's just that most people don't do it like this—I mean...." Now she was blushing. "It's just that I don't want to overdo it. You can do it yourself...."

"I have been. I've been doing it myself."

"You have?"

"I come in here and I take the washcloth and I pee all over it. And it feels good. But I like it when you do it with me."

"Right," she said. "I know."

"I like it when you do it."

"Okay. But tell you what. We'll do it when you're on your period, all right? That'll be kind of self-limiting. If you want to masturbate, on the other hand, do it whenever you want to. I think that's okay."

I sighed. She squatted down in front of me, her hands resting on my thighs. "Come on," she said. "Big Sister knows best."

I reached out and took one of her hands and put it between my legs, with the back of her hand pressing up against my cunt. "Don't move," I said.

She got a surprised look on her face. "All right," she said. Come to think of it, I had sounded a little strange to myself, the way I said "Don't move." But I didn't have time to think about that at the moment.

I closed my eyes for a minute and then started pissing on her hand. "Rub me," I said in the same tone, gritting my teeth.

She gently brushed my cunt with the back of her hand as I pissed all over it.

"Keep doing it," I said. I was holding her wrist with one hand and as she rubbed me, I got that excited feeling again. But I knew I wouldn't piss forever and when I stopped, it would be over. So I held her tighter and rubbed myself faster, finding that increased the feeling. I was breathing fast through my mouth. I rubbed faster, harder, my eyes squeezed shut.

I thought it might feel better if I confessed while I did it.

"I'm peeing on your hand," I croaked. "I'm peeing on your hand while you rub my pussy."

"Yes, you are, Kelly," she said. "Go ahead. It's okay."

"What's okay?" I wanted her to say it too.

"It's okay to pee on my hand. It's okay for you to feel me rub you."

"Rub what?" I wanted all the details.

"To rub your pussy while you piss on me," she said in a shaky voice.

Piss must have been flying everywhere, against my thighs, against the legs of her blue jeans as she squatted in front of me. I groaned out loud. I felt something was building up inside of me. For some reason the words from church came to me, *My cup runneth over.* I wanted to make it run over, but I didn't know how to get there. I felt that if I could run while I did this, it would work.

Now, of course, I know I was trying to come. But I didn't even know what coming was then, and I couldn't make myself do it. When I ran out of piss, I let her hand go and we stopped. Because by now I had it in mind that there was some connection between pissing and the wicked feeling.

I opened my eyes. Julie and I looked at each other. She withdrew her hand, dripping wet, and wiped it off with toilet paper.

Then she bent forward and kissed me on the cheek. "You'd better clean up," she smiled at me, leaving the bathroom quickly.

2

Jason doesn't have a real girlfriend, and he doesn't have a job. He doesn't have any friends, really. All he does that summer, when he is sixteen, is sit indoors in front of the computer, playing games, surfing for porn, doing chat rooms.

One night he's sitting at the computer in his room playing "Warlord II" when Julie comes in without knocking. She's always doing that: coming into his room while he's at the computer, reading, sleeping, talking on the phone. He figures it's her house.

He looks up as she shut the door behind her. She goes and sits down on the bed, while he turns back to the screen because he doesn't want to lose his place in the game. There are about six goblins in the room where he is, and he wants to kill them all before he pauses it. The goblins make growling and screaming noises while he's killing them, and the game's soundtrack music gives a little *ka-bing!* every time one of them dies.

Finally he's able to pause the game. He turns in his chair and looks at Julie on his bed. She's leaning back on her elbows and has kicked off her sandals.

He knows by her pose what she wants to do. Another game—not like the one he has just been playing, but a weird boy–girl game she likes to play. She'd taught him the year before when he was fifteen, and they have been playing it several times a week ever since.

To start the game (he imagines the instructions reading), go into the bedroom of the other person and sit down on the bed. The other person then gets to tell you what to do. That's the name of the game: "Tell Me What to Do." The players must know, or at least pretend to know, what the other wants so that what she makes him do is what he really wants to do.

Fortunately, what he wants from time to time is limited to a few things. And Julie was the one to teach him to talk directly in the first place, to state what he wants so he can get it.

He asked her once if all girls liked to be talked to that way. She'd laughed and said, "Only some girls. You'll have to try to find out."

They sit staring at each other, her on the bed, him in the chair at the computer. She is smiling.

"Unbutton your pants," he says.

She undoes them. They are button-fly jeans so he doesn't have to tell her to unzip.

"Push your pants down just a little. Just so you can give yourself a little room."

She has to use both hands for this, so she lies down on the bed all the way, and shoves the jeans down on her hips.

"Now just put your arms up over your head, and leave your legs like that, with the knees up…that's right."

"Why do you want my arms over my head?" she asks, although she seems to know the answer, because she is already arching her back a little so that her breasts point straight up.

"So I can see your tits." He hears his voice take on the flat, low tone it gets when they're playing this game—kind of like the voice of a cop, who bosses you around without being mad at you because he's done it so many times he can do it without being mad. It's his game face. Jason has a game face now too, and a voice that goes with it.

"Are you looking at my tits?" she asks. "Why are you doing that? Don't you know it's bad to look at a girl's tits?"

"But you're my sister. I can look at your tits anytime I want to."

"How can you say that? That's even worse. It's one thing to look at a girl you want to fuck, but you're not supposed to look at your sister like that."

"What if I want to fuck my sister?" he asks. She sucks in air when he says that, to signal that he's said something that turns her on. When she does that it's like the *ka-bing!* in "Warlord II," to him—like scoring points.

But she protests again, "How can you say such a thing?"

"I say anything I want to my big sister," he tells her. "I do anything I want."

"Oh, no," she groans, but one of her hands is sneaking down toward her pussy.

"Not yet," he says. "Put your hands back over your head. Cross your wrists so it looks like you're tied up there."

She obeys. "It's so bad," she whispers. Her hips are wiggling a little on their own. She thrusts her tits up into the air farther, her head thrown back. "My little brother shouldn't be looking at me like this. You shouldn't see this."

He lets her lie there and wiggle for a few minutes. He is thinking about something he just said, about tying her wrists together. They've never done that, although they've looked at porn online together where girls are tied up, and she's told him she thinks it's hot. Okay, he figures, why not.

He pushes back the chair and stands up. Going into the bathroom—he has his own bathroom because his room is the "master bedroom"—he gets some athletic tape out of a drawer. He stands next to the top of the bed where her hands are resting, the wrists crossed. When he pulls a length of tape from the roll, it makes a sound, *zzhkooooo!* coming off the roll, and she looks up in surprise. He wraps the tape around her wrists.

"Oh, God, what's this?" she says, grinning. He is smiling too.

He gets on the bed and straddles her. First she looks up at him smiling, expectant, but then her face gets serious—not really serious, just sex-serious—and she says, "What are you going to do?"

"What I want," he says, and reaches out his hands. "Look at these tits," he says. He locates the nipples underneath the fabric of her T-shirt from Japantown that reads *Ne plus ultra equals boy trouble!* and begins tickling them. They get hard through the cheap cotton; it makes her gasp again.

"What are you doing?" she protests.

"I'm looking at your tits. And I'm touching them. I'm touching my big sister's tits to see her nipples get hard. They're like pencil erasers."

"What do you know about it?"

"I'm looking at them right now. Can't you feel this?" He tweaks one nipple with the tip of his finger.

"Ook," she whimpers.

"Of course, there's something else we can do to make them hard." He reaches over among the cans, empty and half-empty, of Mountain Dew sitting on the desk next to the computer keyboard, and finds one that has only a few drops in it. He inverts the can and empties the few drops out onto one of her tits. There's just enough soda to soak through the fabric around the upraised nipple. She draws in her breath again. "You like that?"

"So wicked," she says.

He finds another can, this one with a whole mouthful left in it, so that when he empties it out over her other tit, the soda fizzes and drips down her side. She wiggles uncomfortably. "Motherfucker!" she snaps. "It's dripping down my fucking side, it's sticky."

"What do you care? It's my bed."

She thrusts her breasts into the air again. "For God's sake touch me."

"Okay, since you're begging."

She snickers and bucks her whole body underneath him. "Shit!"

He reaches out and starts rubbing her nipples through the now-wet fabric. She moans and thrusts her crotch upward again, but he is sitting astride her hips and there's no way she can rub her crotch against him. "You're gonna have to wait for it," he taunts.

"God dammit," she says. "God dammit."

"Feel this." Still just on her tits. "You like that?"

"Do it harder." He rubs harder, the nipples under his fingertips staying hard in the wet T-shirt. "Harder." He starts scratching with his fingernails, and she cries out.

"Is this what you came in here for?" he ask. "For a little affection from your little brother? Were you lonely?"

"Arghh. Let me touch my cunt."

"Not yet. I'm not done giving you affection."

With a grunt she thrusts her whole body upward and throws him off. Rolling on her side, she swings her bound hands at his face and smacks him hard.

"Ow, fuck!"

"Ha!" she cries. "Think you're big enough to keep me down, huh? Not yet, little boy."

"Fuck, you really hit me."

She sticks a knee on his chest to pin him down and with one bound hand grabs his chin. "And there's more where that came from, so you'd better do what I say." She pushes his head back. "Take my pants down. Down around my knees. I'm not even going to take time to make you undo my hands, because for what you're going to do, I don't need any hands."

He reaches down and pulls down her pants as far as he can reach; she wriggles them down a little farther and manages to kick one leg out. Then she galumphs up to his head. "You'd better not fight back, because I can't balance that well, and I might just crack you again. Now eat my fucking pussy!"

She shoves her crotch forward onto his face. She's got her thighs on either side of his head and he can't hear anything, except from time to time when she hurls her body back and forth, and then he hears her moaning and cursing.

He tries to zero in on the clit, but she's moving around so much, either from arousal or from trying to keep her balance, that it's hard for him to keep a consistent rhythm going. But he tries his best.

It was last summer when they started all this. Their little sister was away at camp.

At the beginning of that summer, all Julie did was lie outside on the patio getting a tan, and all he did was sit inside playing computer games and surfing for porn. He would go on a chat channel and try to act grown up and get chicks to have virtual sex with him. He wasn't very successful because he didn't know much of what sex was about, but by lurking he picked up enough pornographic lingo that it was a bit of an education. He also surfed sites that featured dirty pictures—the ones that had free samples he didn't need a credit card for.

But one evening while he was looking at pictures, Julie surprised him by coming into his room. He would have exited out of Netscape except that he had his hand for the moment on his cock and couldn't move fast enough.

"Stop!" she said when she saw him reach for the mouse. There was silence except for the quiet hiss of the computer. The room was filled with the smell of the suntan oil she'd been using. For a moment she just stood there, looking over his shoulder at the image on the screen.

Then she said, "I see a girl with her face covered with come. She's just finished sucking off a guy, 'cause I can see the cock she's holding, and also in the background I can see part of another guy and his cock. She's doing a scene where she has to suck off a bunch of guys and they come on her face. And you're getting off on it."

Julie reached for the mouse and clicked BACK. Now they were looking at a whole page of small pictures from the same scene. Julie clicked on one of them, and the screen filled with an image of the same girl, still holding the same cock, but turning now to put her mouth around another cock that had entered the frame, while in the background the other guy was still standing there, suggesting there were several guys in the scene.

"That girl's getting to suck a lot of cock," Julie observed. She clicked back to the index page and looked at some of the other small pictures. Then from the index page she clicked BACK again. "Let's see what else you've been looking at."

They were now looking at a page that listed links to dozens of porn sites. Each of the sites was listed with a headline, and it was easy to see the ones Jason had visited, since they had that visited-link color.

"Well, you've been busy today." She started reading off the ones he'd visited. "'White whore sucking black cock,'" she read. "'Big tit girl with red pussy hair.' 'Bizarre dog suck scene.' 'Amateur couple B and D.' Hmm, now you read, Jason."

"Urk," he stuttered.

"Go ahead, Jason. Read me what you've been looking at. Maybe we'll look together."

"'Japanese schoolgirl facials,'" he stammered. "'Lesbian couple and a big dog.' 'Twins in suck scene.' 'Mom tied up by delivery man.'" And he had to read every single link he'd visited, about twenty of them.

When he got to the bottom of the page, he just sat there for a second. Julie clicked randomly on a link and got a page full of little pictures of a middle-aged guy fucking a little blond chick. She snorted and turned away from the screen. "Look at me," she said, standing in the middle of the room. "Turn your chair around. I want you to face me."

She was wearing only her bikini, since she'd come inside from the patio. She reached behind her and unhooked it. "You know why I came in here, Jason? You think I'm checking up on you or something. But to tell you the truth, I'm just kind of horny."

He watched dumbfounded as the bikini top sprang off her tits and they bounced free.

"I'm lying on the patio on that fucking broken chaise lounge," she continued. "And I'm having fantasies about guys, you know? Basically doing what you're doing, only in my head instead of on the screen. And I thought to myself, 'Am I going to just lie here all fucking summer?' And I thought, maybe we can have a little fun. You and me."

She cupped her tits in her hands. "Like this."

He finally found his voice. "Are you kidding?"

"No, I'm not. I'm not that mean. I know it embarrassed you to have me find you like that, and I really didn't intend to, but I was curious. I had the feeling you were doing something like that up here. Boys and their pornography thing. You'll have to show me sometime." She took her hands away from her tits and they bobbed free again. "But really, Jason, why look at it on the screen when you've got the real thing right here?"

She took off her bikini bottom. "Look, little brother. Can you see?" The curtains had been closed to keep out the glare, but there was enough light for him to see his nineteen-year-old sister standing naked in front of him.

"Tell me what you see," she said.

He swallowed and licked his lips. Finally he said, "Petite hot teen with hairy pussy."

She threw back her head and laughed. "That's right. That's me. Petite hot teen with hairy pussy. Now let's look at you." She came over and knelt down in front of him. "Let's get these pants off. The T-shirt too while you're at it. Okay, now we're even."

She backed away a little and stared at him. "They must have porn sites for boys too. What would you be? 'Slim fifteen-year-old with tremendous boner.'"

She reached out for his hand and made him stand up. "Come

here, Slim Fifteen-Year-Old." They stood in the middle of the room, so close he could feel her body heat. Even that summer he was already an inch taller than her. Her hand reached down. "Let me touch it. Hmm, that is some boner. How do you compare with the guys in the pictures, huh? I'll bet yours is bigger."

He looked at her face and felt her fingertips on his prick. Nobody had ever touched him there before, and the sensation was unbelievable. Her fingers trailed up and down his cock, exactly like he had imagined somebody might do someday. They were staring into each other's eyes, and it was so intense he thought he would scream.

"Julie," he said, "should we be doing this?"

"Why not?" she said. "Doesn't it feel good? Do you want to do something else?"

"No, I mean—"

"You don't want me to stop, is that what you mean?"

"No...."

"I'll stop if you want," she smiled, as if she knew no boy in the universe would make her stop at that moment.

"I mean, is this okay to do? Like, brother and sister?"

"Jason, everybody does it. It's in the pornography, right?"

"Well yeah, but—"

"Who do you think those 'twins' are, anyway?"

He chuckled, but the laugh stopped in his throat, because she had now wrapped her hand around his cock and was holding it almost tightly.

"I'll bet it would take so little to make you come," she said.

"Bet you're probably right."

She started to bend down, then smiled up at him again. 'Big sister gives little brother blow job,'" she said. "Got a camera?"

After Kelly came back from her summer camp, they were very careful. They snuck around behind Kelly's back. And they've been doing it, without her knowing, for a year.

Julie is riding his face. She's starting to fuck back and forth, and he is able to get better aim. Then she springs up and, instead of kneeling over his head, she squats over his mouth. She's got a handful of his hair. "Don't stop, little brother," she orders. "I just wanted to watch you do it."

He goes back to work, and she holds her cunt as still as she can. "Look at that boy eating pussy," she croons. "Look at that. Gonna make me come, huh? Gonna make me come?"

"Uh-huh."

"Do it, do it, make me come, oh God…" and with a last hard scattering lick, he does make her come, and hears her moan and whine and gasp and curse while she tugs at his hair.

3

That summer I masturbated a lot. I had nothing else to do, since I was totally bored with going to the mall with girls from school. It seemed so stupid to walk around in a little group with three other girls going, "Oh, he's hot!" or "You're such a virgin!" when I could be home making myself feel good. "Do it whenever you want to," Julie had said. I took that literally, except for going into the bathroom for privacy.

It isn't that I wanted to hide from Julie. She was all I could think of, her and Jenna. I took turns picturing them. I would sit on the toilet, as close to peeing as I could get without actually letting it out, rubbing my pussy and thinking of one of them coming in by surprise.

They'd see me with my fingers touching my pussy, and they'd say, "Kelly! What are you doing?!"

Of course Julie would know exactly what I was doing. It wouldn't be any surprise to her—she's the one who told me I could do it. She's the one who showed me how to do it.

But I would still imagine her surprised face. It didn't matter that in real life she'd touched my cunt, that I had grabbed her hand and pushed it up against my slit and made her masturbate me.

No, that's not quite right. She hadn't exactly done that. All she'd done, really, is put her fingers on my pussy when showing me how to put the tampon in. And then when I'd grabbed her wrist, it wasn't something she was doing, it was something I was doing. It's not like incest or something.

I wondered if Jenna did it too. When I told her that I'd started my period—without telling her anything about what Julie and I had done—she shrugged like it was no big deal. She gave no sign that it meant anything at all to her. So neither did I.

To tell you the truth, it made me kind of sad. Here was this girl I was totally in love with, and just when I got ready to do something about it, suddenly we weren't talking about the one thing that could have made it happen. If I could do with Jenna what I was doing with Julie, I would die from happiness. But I couldn't bring myself to tell Jenna what was happening, especially the part about Julie, and I didn't know how to explain it without talking about her. So I was stuck.

But if I couldn't do it with Jenna, I could imagine it. One day soon after that first menstrual period, I'm sitting on the toilet rubbing myself as usual. It feels good. It feels good when I press the flat of my fingers, the palm side, against my crotch and rub the whole area. I wipe them back and forth across my pussy the way I rubbed Julie's. It feels good.

But then I get to some limit, the place where I'm very excited and ready to piss, but I know there has to be something else. I know enough to know that pissing is not really the goal of masturbation, that there is something called "coming." But I don't know what it's like, and I don't know how to do it. I know it's related to the excitement feeling and that it's called a climax, but that doesn't really help me. Is it like the climax in a movie, where everybody is shooting everybody else in slow motion and inside me there are little thrills as one character after another gets blown away, until the hero is left standing? Or is it like the circuit breaker box in the basement Julie showed me one day, with little levers that get flipped one after another, until you can finally flip the big lever that turns on all the lights? Is that the end? How does it relate to my pussy?

I stand up and go over to the sink, put my foot up on it like Julie did. Only I'm not as tall as her, so I can't really bend my knee much. I just rest my leg up on the counter like a ballet dancer doing stretches. The key thing is to be able to see myself in the mirror. I put my fingers on my cunt again and rub, looking at it in the mirror, but I'm not close enough. I clamber up on the counter, on the area to one side of the sink. I can squat right in front of the mirror, much closer. This is better. I part my cunt lips and really look.

There is hair growing around my cunt. I knew this, but I didn't really know how much was growing toward the lower part, around the bottom—there is a dark fringe. I stare at the hair: It's like a squeal moment in a horror movie when they show the decapitated head in the icebox or something. I can't take my eyes off it, the line of dark hair leading down around my cunt toward my asshole. It's like a line of ants trailing off to a little dark hole. Shocked as I am by the sight, it flips one of those levers in me, and when I start rubbing myself again, making sure not to cover the hair from my sight, the excitement builds higher and faster than it did before. I rub harder and harder, staring at my dark pubic hair, and I say in my mind over and over again, *dark, dark, dark,* and it gets me more and more excited. Then I can feel something inside me releasing and I think I'm going to pee, but I don't, the thing releasing is deeper than that. It's like there's going to be one Big Lever that gets flipped after all the others have been, and I'm afraid I'm going to lose my balance, just let me rub a little longer before I tip over because I really think I'm getting somewhere, dark, dark hole. I can't keep my eyes open any longer, but the image of the dark cunt hair is imprinted on my mind, and then I think of Julie's cunt hair and how much of it there is, and then the Big Lever really does get flipped, big time, deep inside me, a movement. Oh God, her hair all around her pussy. Wicked, wicked to think about it. I am shooting bullets out of my cunt. This might not be good for me, but her hair oh jesus.

Finally I sit down and the cold tile of the bathroom counter shocks my eyes open. What have I done?—surely there must be some uncontrollable bleeding going on. But no. I'm panting. The telephone is ringing in the house. I hear Jason stomp past and into Julie's room and answer it.

I pull my shorts back up and leave the bathroom and stagger down the hallway to my room. There in the darkness, since the curtains are drawn, I flop down on the unmade bed. My cunt is still glowing. I start to stick my hand down there and stop myself. I can't do it in here, where there isn't any lock. I turn over on my stomach. A piece of the twisted sheets and blankets is underneath my cunt, pushing up against it, like a hard knot I can rub against. Without even thinking, I start rubbing my crotch against it; it feels good. Also I realize that by having an orgasm while squatting on the bathroom counter I haven't peed as usual when masturbating, and my bladder is full. I have to go, and this turns me on even more, although I don't dare do it on my bed, of course. I decide that I'll do this for a while, I'll move my crotch against the knotted bedsheets, and then when I really do have to go, I'll just return to the bathroom.

I hump the hard place in the sheets for a while, getting excited. It feels good to move my body to do this rather than just sitting and moving my hand, and while the places the twisted sheet can touch are not as specific as what I can do with my hand, there's an indirect feeling that's sort of exciting on its own, like somebody else is doing it to me. Also I'm thinking about the idea that my piss might possibly dribble out onto the bed before I can stop it, just a few drops probably, but yellow enough to be noticed and definitely embarrassing. My hands grip pillows and sheets, I try to pull on them in such a way as to make the sensations stronger, but it doesn't really help. I shove my face into my bed, I try to rub everything I can. My hips are moving in a way they've never moved before, and the shock of realizing this makes me stop. What must I look like? I roll over onto my back, but the sudden motion just makes the piss in my bladder heave like I'm a walking water balloon. I decide to go to the toilet and maybe make this feeling stop.

I go back into the bathroom and sit on the toilet. One hand in between my legs, back to the place I rubbed before, just above the cunt, where there's a place I guess is the clit, or maybe that's something else—I mean, who knows? It's a little like the hard knot in the sheets, and when I rub it in a certain way, not directly but off to the side a bit, as if I was pretending not to, it feels good. But I'm not thinking of that, I'm thinking about pissing, as I always think when I'm doing this, thinking about spraying my piss out of my body and Julie looking at me, my piss running down her hand, she's looking at me. And wanting to do it to her, wanting to kneel in front of her while she does it, press my hand up against her pussy as she does it, and feel her warm urine coming out.

I almost come, almost piss, almost come, until the piss wins and comes shooting out of me. I stop rubbing my clit and just rub my pussy lips gently and slowly, pretending I'm rubbing Julie's while she does it on me. I imagine her saying "Oh Kelly, oh Kelly," over and over again while I touch her. I would do it really good.

Piss is getting all over my hand. I don't mind at all; I can't even remember when it seemed weird to touch it. But what really turns me on is imagining that it's Julie's piss streaming out of Julie's cunt, that she's doing it on me, saying my name.

4

A Saturday night in midsummer. Julie drives along the franchise strip as the last part of the sunset blazes yellow and purple in the sky, and the big plastic signs light up in all their garish horror: Wendy's, McDonald's, Texaco, U-Haul, Best Western, Pizza Hut—it goes on for more than a mile.

She can remember a short period a few years ago when it seemed like the best possible thing would be for her to get a job at one of these places so that she could make minimum wage, see her friends from high school when they came cruising in, and eat free french fries.

What a joke.

Instead, after about three weeks of taking orders at a fast food place, when she couldn't take it anymore she threw an entire milkshake at a pimply kid in a clip-on tie who was the night manager, and walked out. When she roared out of the parking lot, she smashed right into a Mom-mobile, and changed her life.

It being Friday night at 1 A.M., the mom in question—a thirty-two-year-old part-time hooker named Doreen, who lived in the suburbs but worked out of a motel in South Houston—was on her way back to her split-level from an evening full of blowjobs and quick fucks, her purse full of money. When Julie pulled her tearful oh-God-how-am-I-ever-going-to pay-for-this act, Doreen sized her up and said, "Honey, I know exactly how you're going to pay for it."

Julie was sixteen.

For two years they were a mother–daughter act. Doreen would fuck a guy on the bed, and just as he was coming Julie would wander out of the bathroom wearing nothing but a T-shirt, rubbing her eyes and saying, "What's going on, Mom, I hear noises." And Doreen would answer from underneath the guy, "Mommy's still busy, darling, but if you want to watch, just sit there on the chair and don't bother Mommy and the nice man." Half an hour later, the nice man would be paying five hundred bucks to come in the mouth of "a fifteen-year-old who'd never even seen a cock before." Sometimes the nice man wanted more, but that was all Julie did. If they insisted, Doreen had a .45 in her purse. Doreen took good care of her.

Julie paid off Doreen for the damage to her Windstar in about two months. But by then Julie was kind of hooked on the money, and she was making so much as Doreen's partner that they kept at it, both putting away a few thousand a week. After two years, Doreen retired and Julie went independent. Now that she's legal, she's doing lap dances and handjobs at a primo strip club, and makes more money in a night than she ever did sucking cock. Guys bring her presents, practically throw money at her, just for her to grind her naked pussy on their (clothed) crotches and say it turns her on. That's the easy part—and she doesn't need a gun to keep order, because the club has bouncers. The real work is the emotional manipulation: getting men to give her yet another twenty when she makes like she's going to leave their table, while pretending that if they pay her enough attention (and presents, and money), one day she might actually fall in love with them and give it to them for free. As fucking if.

That Jason, she thinks—he doesn't know how good he's got it.

It's midweek and one of her nights off. She drives along with the window open. Even though it's still hot as blazes out, she needs to clear her head and think about what's going down on the home front.

She thinks: Messing around with Jason is one thing. First of all, as a guy, he's basically just a cock and balls. That is, he's her brother, she loves him and all, but there is little more to him than eight inches and some sperm. She can do anything she wants with him, and if it makes him happy to think he's in charge once in a while, great. In the meantime he's not out fucking some teenage pussy, getting somebody pregnant, and vastly complicating his life and hers.

If that sounds calculating, she does really like Jason's cock. As a sixteen-year-old he's got better equipment than practically anybody she's met at work. Since she's been teaching him to fuck her in the ass, they have some major fun together. She's doesn't have to pretend with him.

But Jason is still just Jason. No matter what she does, he's going to bounce back. She can imagine him thirty-four or even forty-four years old, still skinny and with a giant hard-on, plowing between her legs.

Kelly is another matter, a *way* different pint-sized bomb of another matter, she thinks. Sitting on the toilet, showing me her cunt, pissing on my hand while I diddle her, making her talk about it. I mean, come *on*.

Well, okay—she did start it. Julie's the one who made up that stupid story about how Kelly's pee might be "different" and that she had to watch her do it to make sure. What was that about, she wonders. Where did that come from? And why was it about piss? It's not as if she's into it.

In any case Kelly sure caught on fast. It's obvious she's masturbating all the time, because Julie walks into the bathroom and there's little drops of pee all over—not that Kelly doesn't try to clean up, but she doesn't realize how much she scatters when she masturbates like that.

Part of her knows it's weird, what she's doing with her siblings. Even though she told Jason everybody does it, that was a huge exaggeration. Actually she's only heard once or twice from guys about fucking their sisters, and that was from customers. Customers will tell you anything.

And yet, what she's doing with Jason and Kelly is better than what she herself had. Her first fuck was in the back seat of a Camaro. Her second fuck was a different guy, two days later, who shoved her down on the floor of his closet. And so forth. In comparison, what she's doing with her brother and sister is safer and more loving. At least they'll be able to say their first experiences were with someone who really loved them.

She turns off the main drag and into one of the endless subdivisions, take two right turns, a left, another right at the second intersection, and then it's the fourteenth beige house on the right. If there didn't happen to be a fire hydrant out front, she'd never find it.

The garage door rolls up at her command, and back down again when she's pulled inside. After she turns off the engine she sits for a minute in the dim garage-door-opener light. It's late July, and another month has passed since the last time she'd "helped" Kelly with her menstruation. That means another series of "lessons" are due to start anytime now.

She's wondering how to play it. Surely this pretend-helping thing can't go on much longer. What happens when Kelly drops the pretense and just starts jacking off in front of her or, even worse, reaches for her pussy? Because she knows Kelly's got a thing for her pussy, from the way she looks at it, as avidly as any customer.

She goes inside the house through the laundry room and the kitchen and finds Jason on the couch in the family room, watching an old *Star Trek*. She sits down next to him without him reacting.

They watch until a commercial comes on, and then she picks up the remote and switches to pay-per-view. She punches up a dirty movie, saying, "Young man, that's the last time I want to come into this house and find you're not watching pornography."

He giggles. She has switched on a group-sex video and turned the sound off. A woman about Doreen's age is getting fucked from behind, and has a cock in one hand while some guy is pointing another toward her mouth. In the background, you can see some blond girl in pigtails giving a guy a blowjob.

She puts her hand on Jason's crotch. He's gotten hard watching, or maybe it's just her. She kind of thinks it's the movie, though.

"Take it out," she says.

He unzips his jeans and shoves them down around his ankles. She dangles her fingers across his prick, and he sighs like a contented dog.

He thinks they're so nasty. He doesn't even know what she does at work. As far as he's concerned, she does night accounting for an oil drilling company. One of these days he's going to realize you don't make the kind of money as a night accountant that she must be making to support the three of them.

On the screen, a close-up of a blowjob. The woman sucks her cheeks in, rolls her eyes to look at the guy she's sucking, looks at the camera. She reaches up and grabs the prick with one hand and begins alternating jacking and sucking it.

Jason has his head thrown back, concentrating on her fingers. She jabs him in the ribs. "You're not watching," she says. "We're paying for this. You may as well enjoy it."

He regards the screen. "I'm waiting for the come shot."

"To do what?"

"To fuck your ass, slut."

She laughs.

"Get on the floor. No, go get the lube. Then get on the floor."

"Yes, Mister Suave."

From her room she grabs a towel, lube, gloves, and also a harness and dildo. It's about time for her to be breaking him in, too. Then we'll see who the slut is.

She stops by the kitchen for some paper towels, then strips off her clothes in front of the TV. He's jacking off lackadaisically. "Where's Kelly?" he asks.

"At Jenna's birthday party. She'll be there all night." She gets down on the floor, her ass pointed at him. "Okay, little brother, let's see some action."

He sinks to the floor with a thump. She feels his prickhead nosing around in her pussy hair. "Gonna get it wet?" she asks. "Gonna get your cock wet in your sister's pussy? Big hard cock. Come on, little brother, show me who's got the prick."

"There we go," he says as he finds the hole. He slides it in gracefully, all in one motion.

"Enyuuhh," she grunts. "Man."

"You like that?"

"You know I do."

"Tell me."

"You know I like your nasty cock, Jason, you know I like it when you sink it in my cunt."

"Yes, you do."

"Just don't come, because I'm really feeling like getting fucked in the ass."

"Oh, you are, huh?"

"Yes, and that's where you'd better do it. Hey, I mean it," she says, pulling away. His cock flops out and he laughs.

"Let me put it in one more time."

"No, I want to suck my come off it. Stick it in my mouth."

He is still kneeling on the floor in front of the couch. Both of them turn a little until she can take his prick in her mouth.

And that's the position they're in when she opens her eyes and sees, standing in the dark kitchen, their little sister Kelly. Standing stock still, watching them. Horrified, perhaps. Or riveted.

Julie freezes for just a second. Jason pushes back, wanting her to keep going. He's turned away from the kitchen, and in any case has his eyes closed.

To buy time, she begins actively sucking him again. What the hell does she do? Does she finish him off this way and hope he collapses back against the couch, so that she can shoo Kelly away? She can't let him fuck her in front of their sister. But she's not too wild about Kelly seeing him come in her mouth, either.

She's stuck on this dilemma when Kelly decides it for herself. She comes silently into the living room and sits down on the armchair. So she can see the whole show.

Well, Julie thinks, she's had her chance to back out.

She decides that having Jason come in her mouth is the better part of discretion, or something. She pulls off for a moment so she can start talking to him and, possibly, speed the action. "Jason, baby, I'm sucking your cock."

"Yes," he says dreamily.

"I'm kind of getting off on it."

"Oh, yeah?"

"Mmm—yeah, I kind of want to make you come this way."

"Really? You sure?"

"Mmm-hmm." She sucks him just the way he likes it.

"What about the ass-fucking?"

Oopsy. Well, there was that dildo and harness lying next to them on the floor. She was going to have to explain that eventually, anyway.

"Baby," she says, a strand of saliva connecting her mouth and his cock as she pulls off, "you can fuck me in the ass later. But for now, let's see you come in big sister's mouth."

She glances over at Kelly. Her eyes are as wide as if she were on acid. As Julie wraps her mouth around Jason's cock again, the two girls' eyes meet. Julie winks, and Kelly smiles a little.

So far so good. Now to get it over with. Ordinarily she likes to make Jason wait as long as possible—which, since he's sixteen, isn't very long. For the first few months, all it took was for her to suck his cock for two seconds and *zam!* he'd be coming. Eventually he got a little used to it, so that they can make it last as long as five minutes. She doesn't want him to build up a lot of steam tonight, though, so she decides to pull out all the stops right away. She sucks him and makes sure he can feel her tongue at the same time. She cups his balls just where he likes it, and she makes little groans and grunts in her throat. Sure enough, it gets him going.

"Oh yeah," he starts. "Oh, Julie, that's the way." And he keeps up that way, his monologue building over the course of about a minute, until yes, he comes. Squirting come into her throat, jamming his cockhead against the roof of her mouth, grabbing and pulling at her hair, and saying, "God oh God oh God oh God I'm coming, jesus fucking christ!"

He slows down, his come still spurting, his cock still thrusting, her grunting—grunting for real because she does like it, it does get her off, and even though, or maybe because, she knows that when they open their eyes there's going to be hell to pay, she tries to make it last just a little longer.

How I Adore You

To favor me,
You revealed the secret mystery of the self,
And by your words,
My delusion is dispelled.
                         —BHAGAVAD-GITA 11:1

The bar, in a gentrifying district of artists and cafés, was full of people on a Thursday night. I was there alone; I was going to bars alone, hoping to leave with someone, but everyone else came and went in couples or larger groups. I sat at the bar, wondering if my being alone was going to be a problem for the woman I wanted to meet. I didn't know who she was, but when she showed up, I didn't want to seem like some psycho loner. Solitary, okay; a little aloof, perhaps. But not crazy.

I had been alone for a few years. I could afford to be alone a little longer.

I sat there for an hour when I saw her, sitting with a group of two other women and a man. She was so striking. She was more than just eye-catching—almost monumental—but in the way a marble statue is, one and a half times larger than life, expanded slightly because it stands on a pedestal ten feet high. And yet she was not especially big, although her features were. Her face was like an icon: Looming out of the dark of the bar, it compelled devotion.

She also seemed to have a lazy quality, a reluctance to move too fast or smear her makeup, but her whole being breathed life and warmth and big-boned sexiness—to wit, a broad. She was still. Look at a cloud unmoving at 25,000 feet; look back, it has changed from a flop-house to a palace.

I spied on her in the bar mirror while she talked to her friends. Then they all left, and I went home, cursing myself for not having had the courage to make a move.

The next night I went back again, and she was there in the same spot, talking to someone else. Again I watched her covertly. When she noticed me watching her, I could see her recognize me from the night before—her gaze held mine for a few seconds, and she smiled when she looked back at her companions, this time two men. Then she looked in the mirror at me again.

She went to the bathroom and I followed, washing my hands as she did her business in the stall. When she came out, I turned and she met my eyes. It was one of those moments where it seems like it takes someone ten minutes to walk across a space of two and a half feet, our eyes locked the whole time. I didn't get out of her way and let her have the sink, and she didn't go around me, either. When she finally got to me, I put my hands lightly on her hips.

I expected her to look down submissively, then up at me again. It's what girls do when they want to be kissed. Instead, she looked at me directly. And then she kissed me. A light kiss that got heavier—not too intense, but a real kiss and then some. Her tongue touched mine, that was something. I didn't even know who she was.

Then she told me her name—Elena—and wrote down her phone number.

I spent the next few days in a haze of desire. Oftentimes, early in the fall, there will be a few days in San Francisco that turn warm and dry, more so than all year long. The wind blows from the east, as it hardly ever does, and people get jumpy and nervous. They call it earthquake weather, because there's something about the dry windiness and the building tension that seems to demand a cataclysmic resolution. For those few days it was earthquake weather inside me.

I don't know what I wanted. To worship her iconic face? To have her squash me flat? To throw her up against the wall? Whatever happened, it was going to be momentous.

Finally, a few nights later, we were in her room in the Mission. It was one of those beautiful '20s apartments that have French doors and wooden floors and are situated in a nice building. I knew she hadn't been here that long because she had to be only about 25, and these apartments were now expensive. Maybe she was a trust fund kid.

She gave me a Coke and we sat on her couch. She had a girl folk-rock singer on the stereo. I felt like a teenager sitting there holding a Coke, my hand wet around the sweating can. She didn't even offer me a glass. I sipped because I didn't want to swallow a lot of bubbles and then belch suddenly.

She slipped her shoes off, so I did too. We were about six feet apart, talking about her job downtown at a nonprofit. After a while, I guess she decided a decent interval had passed. She stood up and headed for the bedroom and said, "Come on."

I put the Coke down and followed. I knew we were about to fuck. The idea filled me with an excitement so strong that I was afraid that if I really showed it, she would be nonplussed. So I tried to stifle it and just play it cool.

The moment her tongue touched my mouth, my cunt flashed wet. It was like somebody threw a bucket of warm water on it: one minute dry, the next soaking. Her tongue, sharp and insistent, penetrated my lips and played lightly over my teeth.

"Oh god," I breathed softly into her mouth. She chuckled in her throat.

I was already so turned on but didn't know how much to show. If I tell people how much I want them, how turned on I am and how much I want them to keep doing what they're doing, they tend to think I'm a total nympho psychopath. So I generally try to hide it a little—the "Oh god" was a slip. Maybe I'd wait a little to tell her how good it felt to finally be in her arms, to have her licking my mouth, to smell her body.

I realized my breath was coming in short, panting bursts. She was going to find out in no time anyway. "You're getting me all worked up," I said softly.

"I can stop," she said, smiling, flirtatious. Before I could answer, she filled my mouth utterly with her tongue.

I twisted beneath her. Her mouth was enveloping me and I went into it. My body floated somewhere outside, like a piece of tissue paper curled by a breeze. I wasn't responsible for it.

After a minute, she backed away. I drew a huge breath. "Didn't mean to smother you," she said.

"Smother me," I said, pushing her onto the bed and diving on top of her. I wanted to hold her face in my hands, but instead I found my hands peeling off my jeans and underpants, and then digging my fingernails into her legs, which, if they hadn't still had tights on, might have been damaged in my excitement. I imagined her teeth on my lips; no, I felt her teeth on my lips, so biting seemed the thing to do.

"Unnghh." I found I had clamped my legs around her, so that her hip was mashed up against me—I didn't care, my body was just in a spasm.

When it faded, Elena was looking at me in humorous appreciation. "I don't think I've ever been humped quite like that before," she laughed.

"I don't think I ever did that before."

Her eyes sparkled. "Do you need a second," she said, "or can you do that again for me?"

I laughed nervously. "A second—no, never mind, no time like the present," I said helplessly. "Just kiss me again, that's all I need."

Again with her tongue. My head was swimming, not just with the sensation of being wanted, of being kissed, of having my caresses returned, but at the same time with the conflict of being turned on and simultaneously being a little embarrassed at how quickly I was turned on and yet not wanting her to think I was as much of a slut as I really was.

I forced my hands to lighten up, to stroke her, to listen to her. Once I made myself listen to her and got my spasming body under control, I realized she was a little breathless as well. It was she, after all, who was doing this to me. Her hand was around my throat, I realized.

"Elena," I said, to buy time.

"What?"

"Nothing, I just like saying it. Tell me something."

"What? Stop talking," she said, kissing me again. I didn't want my tendency to overintellectualize to ruin things, so I shut up. Just make out with her, I told myself, even if you did rip your own pants off. Don't get carried away.

I made myself aware of her breath, the undulations of her body. She was peeling back my top now, exposing my tits, which aren't big. She put her mouth around the right one and I let my head fall back, my left hand probing her warm body. "Take your clothes off," I whispered.

While she stripped, I let her look at me, imagining that it turned her on. The same thing that makes me convinced I need to hide my own arousal makes me certain no one could find me very arousing. But, hoping I'll be wrong, I act arousing.

I didn't let myself think she might really like me. I only let myself think she might be turned on.

She finished taking her clothes off and let me put my arms around her. She put her mouth around my nipple again, and I contented myself with letting my eyes roll back in my head and feeling between her legs for something moist. When I found it, she bit down a little. I touched her between the legs, and she did it again. That made for an even exchange for a while. Easy touching, I told myself, gauging it by the strength of her bites.

When she switched breasts, I let a finger slip in. By that point her vagina was really wet, so it was like pushing a finger into a thick soup. I made sure the bites continued.

After a time she pulled her head away. "Jeepers," she said. "What are you doing to me?"

"Not very much," I said lightly.

"Well, keep doing it," she said, closing her eyes. This, this, just looking at her—her heavy olive skin, her thick brows over the closed eyes, her mouth open thoughtlessly—this was enough. Her breathing changed, and I followed it with my touch. It wasn't about making her come, it was about the specific connection between my finger and her breath: the way *this* touch makes her gasp, or *that* touch makes her give a little sound in her throat.

"What?" I said, pressing hard on *that* spot. "What was that?"

She grunted. Every time I touched her, she made that little sound. I don't think it was voluntary. I made sure I wasn't hurting her. No, just doing her clit—rubbing up against the soft, spongy part under the clit itself. The part that makes me...well, never mind me.

"Don't stop," I said. "I won't move. I'm going to keep doing this."

"Unncht," she replied, nodding slightly.

"I just want you to do one thing," I said. "Just put your hand between my legs. You don't have to do anything. Just—" I was seized with a spasm as I felt her hand gently placed on my vagina. "That's right, I just need to feel you there, let me—"

I made sure my finger was still stroking that spot of hers. I thought I could detect a quickening in her. It was so strange, it was as if we were signaling each other from across an ocean, negotiating some alliance of arousal and willingness, even while we were in each other's arms.

"Elena," I said again.

"Sweetheart," she whispered. "Oh, I love that. Just do that."

It was nice of her to say that. I kept doing it.

"Oh, believe me," she said, nonsensically. "Oh."

She came on my hand. I made myself focus on what her face looked like, and on evoking the sighs and gasps that she revealed to me as part of her orgasm this time. I watched it all and took it into me, to the same places that I had to hide from her to keep my own arousal from being seen.

The levels of things not revealed get a little depressing, after a while. So I won't mention it so much anymore, except as an indication of how turned on I was getting versus how turned on I let myself appear. I did let myself wonder if the day would ever come when they approached each other.

So instead: what her face looked like when she came. It was as if an implosion of energy happened, with all her energy drawn into her face and then exploded back out again like sparkly fireworks. Her eyes opened just a couple of times, enough to show how beautiful they were, and then they went back, like the sun setting. Her lips, meanwhile, weren't nearly so poetic; they stretched over her teeth, tightly, in a grimace.

Her voice was doing something.

She finally shuddered, gasping, "Stop!" and holding my hand still against her clit. I obeyed her, and waited while she came back to herself.

Now was the time when she might get embarrassed and pull back, so I made sure not to look too closely at her.

Finally she opened her eyes and smiled at me in a friendly way. What made it strange is that the whole time I was coming on her hand. I was careful not to show it, not to let my orgasm overwhelm hers. Maybe it's not quite correct to call it an orgasm, but really, I was coming, over and over again, into her hand.

I smiled back helplessly. Just do whatever, I said silently to her.

She chose to straighten up over me. I was now on my side a little, one knee drawn up in the air. She pulled me slightly so that I was completely on my back. Then, hope against hope, she lowered her face to my pussy.

Oh man.

She doesn't really want you, I told myself, forcing myself not to grind back against her face. I made my hips dance a very light pattern as she put her tongue against my clit. She doesn't want you, I said to myself over and over again, so don't show her you want her.

"Oh," I let myself say. It meant, Elena, your mouth on me is like the whole fucking ocean. Your mouth is perfect just to look at, and the thought of it, just the thought of your mouth, is enough to make me wet. Just the idea of it being against my pussy is enough to make me come. So what does it mean for you to actually be pressing your lips against me, sucking on my clit, making me do this?

I let my breaths tell the rest of it. My mind went somewhere where she was sticking long needles into my pussy lips in such a way that the pussy was not shut but pinned open widely, so that to be fucked would simply drive the needles deeper into me.

That's the kind of thing I don't let myself say or really talk about.

꒚

No matter how much I tried to talk myself into it while and after we were fucking, I could not convince myself to stay away. I could repeat to myself over and over—and I did, for the next few days—she doesn't want you, she doesn't like you, don't make a fool of yourself by calling first. Or alternatively, you don't like her that much, you don't need her, don't get attached.

It didn't work. I managed to be casual enough in the obligatory next-day phone message, the one you leave at two in the afternoon when you're sure the person is out of the house. But after that, the rule applies: If you really want someone, don't show it for at least the first three dates. And that went double for me. Hide it under a bushel, I would tell myself. She doesn't know how she makes me feel; she doesn't know how excited I am by her eyes and the color of her skin, her black hair and the color of her pussy. Perhaps if she knew, she really would think I was crazy.

So I left fewer messages, sent less e-mail. I gave myself a rule of at least four days between contacts. We went out a few times in the next month, usually ending up back at her place, although once we did it, shivering, in the back seat of my car up on Twin Peaks, under cover of a howling fog. I didn't show her how I felt, I didn't invite her over to my place, and I didn't tell her much about myself. I let my hands and my mouth show her as much as I dared, which wasn't nearly as much as I was thinking and feeling.

She really had me. It got to where I would positively suffer after seeing her. What I wanted to do was camp out on her doorstep, follow her around town, kidnap her to the desert. I wanted to write valentines, make her tapes of my favorite songs, send her a picture of my cat. I had it bad.

Finally, a month had passed, and I figured it was time to show just a little more—not too much. So I left a message in which I told her a little bit about the exact taste of her pussy juice, and how I was thirsty for it, how I would die if I didn't get more of it. She shouldn't wash, she shouldn't wipe herself after peeing, I wanted the exact taste of her cunt the way it was all the time, and then I wanted to make it flood with come so that the taste would be the same and wetter and completely pure.

Ten seconds worth of her voice on the outgoing message, thirty seconds of me babbling about her pussy, and I told myself that might be it for that week's contact with Elena. Although I had left the message in late morning, I deliberately went out that night so as not to drive myself crazy waiting for the phone to ring. I couldn't go to the bar where we'd met, of course, in case it was her favorite hangout—she had been there two nights in a row when we met, after all—and if we ran into each other, it would seem like I was stalking her. Or, worse yet, she would be there with another date, and I would want to kill the world.

I went someplace I figured she would never go, or ever hear of. Over in the Berkeley marina there's a Ramada Inn with a bar where all the closeted lesbians of the East Bay go. It is the least cool, most dorky dyke bar in the whole world, and it's full of square, closeted dykes with awful haircuts—junior high phys. ed. teachers from Vallejo, lady naval officers, Napa Valley wives wearing horrible turquoise mock turtleneck sweaters from Land's End. I put on my most suburban outfit, a camel-colored leather coat and black leggings, went there, and sat on the edges.

By 10 P.M. my new best buddy was the Republican mayor of a suburban community whose husband thought she was working late on city business and who thought it might be daring, some day, to go into San Francisco to a real lesbian bar. She actually told me her favorite book was *Delta of Venus* and said she wanted to go to my "secret place." I asked if she had a secret place of her own in the neighborhood, and we decided to check into the motel.

She hid in the bar while I got the room, of course. I was pretty sure she wouldn't be there when I came back with the room key, but she was.

We went up to Room 219, and I opened the door. The dampness of the room was covered with a full can of air freshener, and I didn't know whether to turn on the heater or open a window. Madame Mayor pushed me onto the bed and started kissing me, and we went on from there. She took off her blouse to shove her sizable tits in my face, and then immediately dove for my snatch. She was more interested in going down on me than vice versa, and I have to say that she did seem to know what she was doing, once she got down to business. Lying there, my tights tangled around our ankles, her in her bra and me still with my coat on, I reasoned that while her husband probably ate her out as much as she wanted, this was the one thing she never got a chance to do. And she gave it everything she had, so I felt the least I could do was fake an orgasm.

Then it was time for her to get back to hubby and the kids. She left so fast I hardly even had time to pull my pants up. The door of the room shut behind her, and I collapsed back onto the dank polyester bedspread, hearing her heels clomp away down the concrete walkway. Her spit was dribbling out of me and I lay there wondering whether the nasty sensation was possibly one saving aspect of the situation. I initially figured she had been degraded more than me, since I had had a fake orgasm and not a real one. But she hadn't even taken her clothes off, while I showed her my secret place, and on my scorecard the one who takes her pants off first is the real bottom. Plus I had been stuck for the cost of the room. Which is really the way Republicans are—they make you pay for the pleasure of getting screwed, and, on top of it, you have to pretend to like it.

Lying there, I had a degradation fantasy in which I went back to the bar the following week and tried to pick her up again, only to have her reject me and go home with a Cal economics Ph.D. I would make a fool of myself following them out to the parking lot, where a pickup truck full of marines would call me "dyke bitch" and throw beer cans at me while the mayor and her new paramour went off in a black Z3.

Then I got up and went to the bathroom and took a shower. When I checked my cell phone, there was a message from Elena. "Hey Susan, it's Elena," she said in her pretty voice. "I thought it was time we saw each other again. You've got my number." Yes, I did. I had it set on number 1 speed dial. And I invited her over for dinner.

꒰

She came bringing sunflowers and an amazing corn chowder. I fixed pork chops, and was gratified when she said, "Pork chops, thank god. I get so tired of lesbian vegetarian cooking."

"Careful, they might hear you," I said. We were standing in the kitchen while I tended the chops, and she leaned against the sink, drinking red wine. Her presence filled the room; she was just as monumental in my apartment as in her own. It wasn't easy to concentrate on the cooking; all my thoughts tilted toward her gravitational force, and I had to force myself not to stare at her and grin sheepishly.

As usual, she gave no sign she noticed my self-consciousness. Her ankles casually crossed, she made small talk about something going on at her job—a new director whom nobody liked, the loss of a grant, the visit of a celebrity. I didn't really care what she was saying; I loved listening to her voice.

Her glance swept the kitchen while she talked, but this didn't worry me. Although I had let down my guard enough to invite her over, I had cleaned madly before she arrived. I had taken down the refrigerator-magnet poetry I'd been composing for her, and the bar napkin with her phone number, on which I had drawn a map of Canada with her face sketched on it twice, was safely filed away under *E*. My kitchen looked like one in a display home.

"So what have you been up to lately?"

Other than pining for her and tricking with a junior Republican, I didn't have much to say for myself, and I wasn't about to mention either. "Oh, just, you know, going to the gym and all."

"Oh, let me see." She put down her wine glass, came over and stood behind me and put her hands on my shoulders. "Kind of muscular here...."

"Oh, yeah?" I chuckled lightly over the ringing of alarm bells. "You'd better be careful, I'm dealing with hot grease here."

She moved her hands over to my biceps. "Ooo, these are nice too."

"Elena...."

She didn't heed my warning. She ran her hands up and down my arms, down my back, and started to put her hands under my sweater. "Nice..." she cooed.

That was too much to bear. I dropped the spatula in the pan, spun around, and pulled her roughly to me, crushing her breasts against mine. With one hand I yanked open her blouse; one of the buttons flew into the lettuce that was draining on the sideboard. She was wearing a frilly red bra. "So are these," I said.

I ripped the blouse open wider, tore a bra strap off her shoulder, pulled out a tit, and sank my teeth into it.

For each movement she went gasp! gasp! gasp!, throwing her head back when I bit her. Then one final gasp as I shoved her back to the sink.

Inside, I was thinking, well, that was perhaps a little extreme. But I didn't bite her hard.

She seemed kind of shocked for a second. Then she laughed a little. "Big meany," she laughed, rearranging her bra. "I haven't been treated like that since I made out with the captain of the girls' volleyball team in high school. What came over you?" she said, still laughing, trying to button her blouse and realizing she was missing a button.

I decided I should make a joke of it. "Must have been those sunflowers you brought," I said. "I have Van Gogh's Syndrome. I see sunflowers and I go nuts. Your button's in the salad," I added.

She laughed. "'Van Gogh's Syndrome.' You're crazy."

I turned and shook the spatula at her. "Don't call me crazy, don't call me crazy!" I said in a crazy voice.

"You kill me," she said. "There it is. I'm putting this in my coat pocket so it doesn't get lost."

We managed to eat dinner in peace. We killed a bottle of wine, and she kept laughing at everything I said. I even told her about the

Republican mayor—pretending it had happened two years before instead of the night before. "I didn't know you were so funny," she smiled.

"I'm not funny, I'm crazy."

"Yes, you are."

Crazy about you, I thought. But I didn't say it because by then she would have thought it was just another joke.

We moved to the couch. This is where the scary music would start on the movie soundtrack, I thought. "You gonna be mean to me again?" she asked.

"I don't know. Depends how mean."

"Crazy mean."

"Oh, don't say that. That's too mean."

"Yay, crazy mean!" she laughed. She must be a little drunk, I realized.

I sprang across the couch, put a knee between her legs and my hand around her throat, but I did it all gently, not rough like before. Pushing my face up to hers, I said, "Elena, you don't know what you're asking for. You don't know crazy mean. What I did before was fun mean. I think that's what you want, isn't it? The fun kind of mean? Because I love you too much for the other kind."

She looked at me, her neck resting in my hand, thinking about it, while my words echoed in my ears. I had blurted it out, and now all my carefulness had been in vain. Now she was going to turn sarcastic, fuck me but not let me fuck her, and then our next meeting was going to be in a café where she would tell me she wanted to slow things down. My intestines lurched while I wanted. At least a minute ticked by.

Finally she asked, in a quiet voice, "Did you love her as much?"

"Who?" I asked, tightening the grip on her neck.

"The girl you were crazy mean to."

I looked at Elena's face, which I had spent so much time over the past week dreaming about. I knew she could see the need in my eyes, but now it was too late to hide.

"It's more complicated than loving somebody as much," I said finally.

She looked back at me steadily, no longer silly or drunken. "I guess it's more complicated than being mean, too," she said.

"Yes, it is." I relaxed my grip and let my hand drop, backing away a little.

She took hold of my shirt and pulled me back. "Hey, stay close," she said.

I came closer, but I was tense. I looked down nervously, saw the gap in her blouse where the button was gone.

"Look at me again," she said. "Now what was that you said a minute ago?"

I looked away and licked my lips.

"Go ahead and say it."

"Can't," I mumbled.

"Hmm."

"I know we just met, but.... Aw shit, do we have to talk about it?"

"You started it," she smiled. "But look, I won't hold you to anything. I just want you to do one thing for me. Whatever you started doing in the kitchen, shoving me around like that—I don't care where it comes from or what you call it—fun mean, or S and M, or whatever. It felt real. So do it to me again."

"You sure? You don't seem like a bottom to me."

"I'm not," she said, picking up my hand and putting it back on her throat. "I'm not a bottom at all. But I want you to do what you want."

"Like this?" I said, tightening.

"Like that. Like that and everything else."

I put my other hand around her throat and squeezed gently, the words "crazy mean" echoing. I thought of Kathy, lying with me on the couch in the front room of her flat, asking me to do it to her, telling me to find the carotid and very gently and slightly cut off the flow of blood, telling me that if I could get her just between the point of dizziness and the point of passing out, she would come.

Don't try that at home. She knew what she was doing. I had no intention of going that far with Elena. I felt for her carotid and purposely avoided it, as you're supposed to when you do this. I just choked her a little, cutting off her breath. She looked back at me the whole time, her eyes narrowing to slits, breathing only when I let her, and licking her lips. All her attention on her breath, all my attention on her breath and the way she looked. This is the way I adore you, I said to myself, with my hands around your beautiful throat.

I squeezed tighter, held it, and released. Over and over again, controlling her breath. When, in the middle of a fifteen-count, her hips started moving and her back began undulating, I shoved her down farther on the couch so that she was resting on pillows with her head near the armrest. She took her next breath almost crying. With my left hand I kept the pressure on her throat; with my right I took her chin between my thumb and forefinger.

"Everything else?" I said.

"Susan," she said recovering her voice, "a girl who's not-a-bottom says to you 'Do everything.' Now what do you think that means?"

"That's what I'm wondering."

"It's not going to be top and bottom between us, Susan. It's just going to be real. Now go ahead and do what you're thinking."

"You don't know what I'm thinking."

"Do you want a safeword or something?" she jeered.

I released her chin and slapped her hard three times: palm, back of hand, palm. She cried out. I grabbed her chin again. "That's what I was thinking, bitch!" I yelled.

"And what else?" she hissed right back at me. "What else are you thinking? And when do you stop thinking and just do it?"

"Shit!" I shouted in frustration. I wanted to throw her across the room. So I did. I pulled her up off the couch and tossed her against the wall and sprang after her, thumping into her and making her grunt. She raised her hands as if to struggle; I caught one wrist and slapped her again. Then I dug my hand in between her legs. She was wearing silk trousers, and I could feel lace panties right through them. That had felt good, to put my hand roughly between her legs, so I did it again, and then again, so that it was almost like I was slapping her pussy.

"You're hurting my wrist," she said between clenched teeth. I let up the pressure a little. "I didn't say stop," she immediately replied, so I clamped down again, and harder, making her whimper.

"God-fucking-dammit," she choked. I slapped her again.

"I'm getting to like that," I said, slapping her on one cheek, then the other—not too hard. "It makes my cunt wet to hit you."

"Then," she said between slaps, "I guess...I'd better get... used to it."

I threw her back onto the couch so that she was more or less sitting up. I grabbed a handful of her hair and made her bend down so far that her head was between her knees, not so much because I wanted her to see what I was doing, but because it was the only thing I could do to keep hold of her while I did what was coming next. I crouched down on the floor and, growling like a dog, untied the laces of her boots with my own teeth. I had to release her hair to pull the boots off. Then I threw her on the floor and ordered, "Get your pants off."

She stripped them off. "Not the underpants," I said. "Let's see what you've got for me here." The panties matched the frilly bra, of course. "What a little femme you are."

"Femme, but not a bottom."

"Yeah, right." I stood up and put my shoe on those pretty underpants, resting it on her pussy. I wished I had been wearing giant hiking boots just so their touch on her cunt would be rougher. "Let's see the matching bra, Miss Babe," I sneered. "Let's see the outfit you put together for me."

She unbuttoned the blouse and let it fall open. She ran her hands lightly across her covered breasts. "That's right, keep touching them," I said. "Show me how pretty you think they are. Show me how, when you put that bra on tonight, you imagined me touching them."

She laughed nervously and obliged. Smoothing her hands on the underside of her breasts, she started rubbing her nipples with the flat part of her fingers. She looked so good it made me want to hit her again, but I simply stepped harder on her pussy.

"That's right, show me. Hmm, you're not bad at that. Have you ever been a stripper?"

"Yes."

"Like half the dykes in the Mission. Keep it up. Your nipples are hard, I can see from here."

"Damn right they are."

"And is your pussy wet?"

"Yes."

"Say it."

"My pussy is wet under your feet, Daddy," she ventured.

"Oh, my. I don't know if you want to go there. Let's just keep it real. You call me by my name, and I'll call you a fucking whore. How's that?"

"Susan, you call me anything you want."

That gave me a pang in my cunt. Actually there had been several pangs up to this point, but that was a big one.

"Elena," I said, "Fucking slut, cunt, whore. Elena."

"Yes, that's me," she said. She arched her back into her tits. "This is making me feel so turned on. Are you going to hit me again?"

"Of course."

"Are you going to fuck me?"

"I'm going to hit you, fuck you, whip you, and, as you said, do everything."

"Good, good, good."

I gave her pussy a last kick and she grunted. I grabbed her by the hair and said "Crawl" and dragged her down the hall faster than she could crawl, so that she stumbled and whimpered and bruised her knees. I sat on the bed and made her take off my shoes and socks. When it came time to take off my pants, I told her to take the belt off and coil it on the bedside table. But before she could pull my pants down, I kicked her onto the floor again.

"This is where I wish I had a dick," I said. "This is where you'd suck my cock."

"Susan, I'll suck your cock," she smiled, flinging her hair away from her face.

"And I'd come right in your mouth."

"Yes," she said evenly.

"You say yes because you think you don't have to do it. What if I call my upstairs neighbor down here? He's a twenty-nine-year-old asswipe car mechanic, and every single weekend I have to listen to him fucking right over my head. He must have a dick the size of Texas. How would you like it?"

"Yes," she said. "Whatever you say, I'm saying yes."

I stood up and went over to her on the floor, grabbed her by the hair, and shoved her face into my crotch. "You're a cocksucker, is that it?"

"Yes, I'm a good cocksucker."

"You dig the feeling of a cock in your mouth?"

"Yes, I love cock."

"And you call yourself a dyke."

"Yes."

"Okay, bitch, now only answer 'yes' if it's the truth. Do you really like sucking cock?"

She raised her head and our eyes met. "Once in a while," she grinned.

"You suck!" I laughed.

"Yes."

"I didn't mean it that way."

I shoved her away and took off my own pants.

"You think you're going to get to suck my pussy? Guess again."

I took a scarf from a drawer and tied her hands together and then tied her ankles with another scarf, so she was kneeling, bound, on the floor. "Come here, not-a-bottom."

I dragged her over next to the bed, and I bent over it, leaning on my elbow. I stuck my ass in her face and said, "Eat my asshole, not my pussy. While you do it, I'm masturbating."

She did it without hesitation. Pretty good, too. With her tongue in my asshole I made myself come on my hand and stopped myself from crooning her name only by saying, "I'm coming, you fucking bitch," over and over.

When we were done, I flopped on the bed for a second, then rolled over to the edge and looked at her on the floor. Her face was red from being slapped, her makeup was smeared, and tears were in her eyes.

"You look so good. Do you know that people look better all messed up than they do all put together? That's what I want to do, I want to mess you up. That's the picture I want of you."

"So you're taking pictures?"

"If I want," I said—although I had no way of taking pictures. "Tell the truth. Have you ever licked someone's asshole before?"

"No."

"Good, I finally found a cherry. What else…. Have you really been a stripper?"

"I *am* a stripper."

"And a whore?"

"Not yet. Is that your fantasy? Do you want to be my pimp, Daddy?"

"God," I laughed. "Here I was trying to hold back all this time. I never thought I would find somebody as dirty as I am."

"I'm pretty dirty."

"Does anything bother you?"

"Sure."

"What?"

"I don't know. I'll let you know if you ever get there."

"Tell me."

"I won't. I can't. I'm just telling you some things bother me. I don't know what they all are."

"She said, sitting on the floor all tied up," I mocked her.

"Yeah, and you're making skidmarks on the bedspread."

"You're a smart-ass bottom."

"I'm not a bottom."

I grabbed the belt from the bedside table and let it uncoil in the air. I brought it down in her direction, and she took it on the back, making a little cry. That felt so good I did it again, and then again. There's a satisfying *whoosh-whack* sound a belt makes when you hit somebody with it, if you hit them hard enough, and that sound is one reason I like to do it. And the noise the other person makes is another reason, because they don't control the sounds, the sounds just come out. I paused while I undid her bra in the back, exposing the whole olive field of her torso.

"So you'll let me know when you get there, huh?"

"Yes! Owgh!" she yelled as I hit her again.

"How about it? You there yet, not-a-bottom?"

"Not even close. Oowwgh! God!" She was crying now.

"No?"

"Ow! Fuck. Susan, it's not about where I am, it's about where you get to."

That stunned me. Then I hit her harder.

"Fuck you, not-a-bottom. You let me worry about where I get to."

"I am. Can I masturbate while you do this? Look at me, touching my cunt for you. Now hit me again. Ow!"

"Christ, you do look good like that. That's right, do yourself."

Kathy, spread out on her kitchen table. The table was just the right width for her to hang onto the other side and expose her whole back to me, while the edge of the table on this side was right next to her cunt, and she would rub herself against the edge and come while I was whipping her. She would cry and moan and say in her low orgasm voice, "I'm coming, I'm coming, keep hitting me, don't stop, don't stop, I'm coming, you bastard."

Elena masturbated and I decided I wanted to draw blood at least once. So I lit into her hard and fast four times. She screamed at the end, but four was my number anyway. With satisfaction I watched jewels of blood well up along the lines on her back.

The thing is, she kept masturbating, even after I dropped the belt. Crying, she opened her eyes and turned her head to me. "Look at me," she said, her hand working furiously. "Look at me. Is this what you want? You can have it. Tell me this is what you want."

"This is what I want," I whispered. "I want you just like this. There's blood on your back, Elena. I want you just like this."

"Then we're there, baby," she said, the tears drizzling down from her face. She seemed like she was going to come, but then she slowed and stopped. The room was very quiet then, with only the sounds of our breaths.

When her breath slowed, she sat up, her legs folded beneath her, fetching in her bonds. "God, that was hot. I almost came." She threw her hair back over her shoulder again.

I looked at her, shaking my head. "You are something else."

"My limits are not that physical," she said.

"Oh really?"

"Whipping isn't one of them. You can do that."

"What about your strip-show customers?"

"I can wear costumes that hide the back. The back is not what they're interested in. You shouldn't bruise my ass or my thighs, though."

I smiled. "I don't believe you. Are you for real?"

"Too real, daddy-o."

"You keep going back to that. Have you had a daddy? I mean, a dyke daddy?"

"For a little while. But, and I hate to say this, she wasn't any good at it. But have you ever been a dyke daddy?"

"Sort of."

"It seems to fit you. Not in that porn way. You just seem like a nasty daddy."

"Oh yeah?"

"Who else slaps you and calls you whore and beats the living shit out of you? Daddy."

I was respectfully silent. "Did that happen to you?"

"No, of course not, or I couldn't go there with you. My father was a high school teacher. He loved his students and he loved his kids. He never raised a hand to them, or me."

"That's nice. So why do we do it?"

"I guess we just need to," she smiled.

Another image came to mind of Kathy, her wrists tied, squirming underneath me on a hotel bed in Berlin. I had told her I wanted to burn her with my cigarette, and she was positively terrified. I brought the cigarette closer and closer to the skin of her belly. She was crying and wailing and begging me not to. I had never seen anybody so completely lose it. She was so scared that she shit in the bed.

Then I burned her.

It turned out that what I liked best was the panicky fear, not the burning or the shit, although the combination of them all was pleasingly intense. So after that, I didn't need to burn her every time. I just needed to make her think I was going to. Of course, I had to go ahead and do it once in a while, so that the fear would stay real.

Naturally, she started thinking that there was some reason why I would burn her some times and not others. That I would burn her as punishment for something she had done, so that she would try to do everything right, knowing the moment would come anyway, and then hope that whatever she had done was enough to forestall the actual burning, which she never got used to and which she never lost her fear of.

But the fact is that it had nothing to do with punishment. All it was about was bringing us both to that razor's edge of desire and pleasure on one side and terror and shit on the other. I wanted her to get there, and I wanted to be the one to bring her there.

And the saddest time was when she really had done everything right, when she had done everything I'd asked, to the letter and beyond, when she had cut herself and hacked off her own hair and done everything degrading I could think of. And we both knew it, we both knew that she had done everything perfectly and that she did not deserve to be burned.

So, of course, I had to do it.

Lying there looking down at Elena, at the blood welling up on her back and the tears rolling down her cheeks, I tried to think of the next thing to do. If I could think of something else to do, we could just keep going and come and come and come until the dawn came, and then sleep like the dead. But I couldn't think of what to do next.

The silence went on for so long that she said, "I know we're not done. I don't want us to be done, not by a long shot. I want this to go on and on, because I want you to get to the end of what you're showing me. I want you to show it all to me."

I could not believe her. "No you don't," I said.

"I don't? Suppose you did," she persisted, still sitting tied on the floor. "Suppose you did take it to the end. And at the end I was still not a bottom. At the end you still did not own me."

"What are you saying?" I heard my voice quiver.

"What would it prove? How tough you are? How dirty? I'm as tough and as dirty as you are, I think. What if you've met your match?"

I couldn't speak.

"And if I go that far with you, and you still don't own me, it doesn't mean I'm holding myself back. It would be real. Top and bottom is a fantasy, Susan. This is real. You really tie me up and hit me and call me names. And when I do it to you, it's just as real. It's not switching, it's not role-playing. It's you hitting my face because it makes your arm feel good."

"Yes," I said. "It does. It makes my arm feel good."

"I know. I know more about you than you think. You think you can hide it from me, but you can't. Even though you're holding back, I can feel it, I can see it."

"You can?"

"Yes. So say it."

I couldn't stay up on the bed anymore, so I slid to the floor beside Elena. She scooted a little closer to me but no farther.

"I'm still not untying you, even though we're processing."

"Fine with me. I like being this way with you. Now tell me."

"I love you," I said in a guttural voice that might have sounded crazy. "I adore you. I want you so much, Elena. You make the sun rise on my body. You give me dreams and chills and make me want stuff I don't even want to think about because I know I'll never get it!" I hit the bed in frustration. "Fuck! You only say you won't let me own you because you don't care. You'll do all that shit with me but you don't love me! So what's the point!"

"What's the point of owning me?"

"Because the only way I can own you is if you give yourself to me. And the only way you give yourself to me is if you love me. So you don't love me, fine. I never asked you to!"

"You ask me to every time you look at me."

"Oh, fuck you!"

"Now you tell *me* the truth. Who was the crazy mean girl?"

"Fuck you!"

"You'd better tell me. Because if you don't, then I'll know that whatever you do to me, it's not real."

I swallowed hard. "Elena, I've never told anybody."

"Tell me."

I took a huge breath.

"Kathy. I knew her four years ago. I met her in a bar, like I did you, and we connected like fire and gas. Everything we did was perfect. She went so far with me. Even the stuff that scared the shit out of her, she did. Because she loved me."

"And?"

"We were burning up the world. It was all so real. And what was real is that I had the right to do all that shit to her because she gave herself to me."

"And?"

"One day I made a mistake. I broke her jaw. And that did it. It was like we both snapped out of the place we'd been in for two years. And she had to leave. It wasn't all sudden or anything. We both talked about it. She said it was the limit that she didn't know she had, that if bones were going to start getting broken, she was finished.

"And I agreed. She was right. I didn't mean to break her jaw. I was just out of control for a minute. And I didn't want to be out of control. In a way I deserved it. Like if you kill somebody with your car and it's an accident, you still go to jail.

"I took care of her while she healed up, I waited on her hand and foot for three months. I apologized and repented and abased myself, and we talked and talked, and in the end she was healed and it was over."

After I was silent for a minute, she asked, "How did you break her jaw?"

Now I did bury my face in my hands. I didn't want to look at her while I said this. "Just by being rough. By hitting her."

"With your hand? Just whack?"

"Yes. I was in a state. I was all wound up. We had been fucking for hours and I hadn't come and I was so high on endorphins and on sex and on the whole idea.... She was like my toy—or, no, like my exercise mat. She was something I could thump again and again with abandon. Throw my whole body against. I need that. I need someone I can throw myself on, somebody who will catch me over and over, who will accept all my blows and all my kisses, everything I can give. So I did. I thumped her again and again. And then she broke."

Elena sighed a little, taking this in. "Okay. I have to ask you one more thing."

I raised my head and looked at her, smeary and disheveled, her bra dangling from her wrists, tied up with red scarves, but with eyes as deep as the sky.

"In that moment, when you were swinging your hand at her for the last time—in that one moment, how did you feel?"

I stared into her eyes for a long time. I tried to speak but I couldn't. I thought that if I could just fall into her eyes, it would be all right, that once inside there everything would be all right. But to do that I had to say one word, and it was so hard to get out.

But finally I said it. "Happy. Ecstatic. I was going to come soon. She was about to come. I needed to make my arm feel good just a few more times."

And I fell into her eyes.

"Did you want to hurt her, I mean really hurt her?" she asked.

"No. No, I loved her. I didn't want to hurt her. Not really."

"There wasn't something you were pissed off about that day? You weren't secretly punishing her for something?"

"No, no. That's not how I get angry. If I'm really angry I don't show it. I withdraw. Not frozen-type withdrawal, just friendly and distant. Businesslike. That's when I'm really mad. When I'm hitting someone is when I'm happy."

"Okay."

At this she finally moved closer, and had to come up on her knees, but was able to put her head on my shoulder. I touched her head.

"Thank you for telling me that."

"I know it sounds like I totally abused her," I said in a guilty rush. "Like I'm a batterer or something."

"I understand. Is there anything else?"

"It's all I have to say," I said. "That's really all. I told you I adore you and I told you what I did. Those are the two things I felt I could never say to you."

"Yes."

"I needed one other human being on earth to understand the way it was between us." And now I finally started crying, really crying.

"I know."

"Oh, God," I cried. "I give you everything, Elena. I belong to you."

She let me cry for a while, and then raised my head so we could look at each other. "You don't," she said. "You revealed yourself to me. That's a lot. It's like giving yourself to someone. But it's not the same as them owning you."

I looked up at her. Adoration of the icon of her face.

"You revealed yourself to me. That's so valuable. But I do not own you."

I took some deep breaths and stopped crying. I felt too happy.

"Don't hold back with me, Susan. Don't break my fucking jaw, either. But don't hold back."

I untied her and we got on the bed and fell into each other's embrace. Her kisses tasted like my ass, and her back was a mess that I would have to clean up, and there was still so much to do, but now all I needed to do was hold her and listen to her say, "You revealed yourself to me."

Prom

Me and Crazy Janey were makin' love in the dirt,
Singin' our birthday songs.
                              —BRUCE SPRINGSTEEN

1

It's Prom Night.

I'm in my bedroom at home, dressing for the prom. I have a rented oatmeal-colored tuxedo. Last Saturday the formal wear shop at the mall was a controlled riot of seniors, getting fitted at two-minute intervals. You get measured and pick out your color and boom, you're hustled outside by giant armed guards. The shop doesn't want a recurrence of the incident two years ago, when the place got so packed with kids that the plate-glass windows broke from the sheer pressure, some kid bled to death, and sixteen were trampled. Now they have things under control.

I put on the tuxedo, fumbling with the cufflinks and the other unfamiliar components. I straighten my bow tie in the mirror, listening to Incest on the stereo, singing along with their latest hit, "Better You Than Me," when I notice my mother's in the doorway watching me.

It bugs me but she's got the right. She's always spying on me, pretending to surprise me while I'm taking a shit and then staring at me while it plops out of me, or listening to me talk on the phone to my friends. I don't like it, but what can I do about it, she's my mother. Until tonight.

At the beginning of the school year, there were 499 seniors in our class at Burns High School. Since the first day of school, nine killed themselves, three were murdered (one by a gang of other students, who were then subtracted from the class by the authorities), and eight left to go someplace else. Of the nine who killed themselves, four were part of a suicide pact, in which two male–female couples gassed themselves in their car listening to Black Sabbath because the girls were pregnant, and three other suicides were copycats from that. Then there were two unrelated suicides, although one might have been a murder.

They burned, as we say. When someone dies we say, "Tommy burned on Saturday night" or whenever. There is an implicit admission that, eventually, we will all burn.

It's a long time since you went to high school.

Tonight the 472 surviving kids in our class are going to party at the Hyatt Regency in downtown Houston. We've been looking forward to this for a long time, because this night—and not our official graduation—marks the end of our childhood abuse.

Burns looks peaceful, prosperous, well-adjusted. On the surface we follow the form as well as anybody on TV. If you drove along the curving streets, you'd see people mowing their lawns and washing their cars, or talking across the back fence to one another about how much the value of their houses has increased since they bought them.

The people who live here are utterly typical: They cheat their employers, they sexually abuse each other, they buy and sell illicit drugs, and they secretly doubt the American Dream. For most of the wives, marriage is one long rape. Most of the kids in the school get fucked by their parents and older siblings from an early age. Never mind the sheer physical abuse, because if you've survived by the time you get to high school, i.e., by the time you're big enough to hit back, it's mostly over. Parents would never hit you if they thought they were going to get hit in return because they're cowards who only beat up on people smaller and weaker than themselves.

By tradition, Prom Night is the end of it: After tonight, our parents aren't allowed to beat us or fuck us anymore. Unless, of course, you dig it and want it to continue, which is understandably rare. Maybe it would be more accurate to say that Prom Night marks the time when you get a choice.

I notice Mom's got that addled expression on her face. Her mouth is set in a thin-lipped line; her eyes are staring. I recognize this; it means she's turned on. It turned her on watching me put on my pale-brown tux. It's not unusual for me to see her like this; I know all about what she looks like when she's turned on. What's unusual is that my mother is wearing a prom dress.

"Baby," she says, breathing heavily.

"What are you wearing a prom dress, for, Mom?" I take off my jacket and put it on a chair, then go to my desk and take out my gun. It's a .38 semi-automatic she got me for my sixteenth birthday so we could go out together, which we don't do much anymore. I put the gun on the desk and take my shoulder holster out of the drawer and put it on over my head.

"I want to be your date."

"I've already got a date, Mom."

"That little cunt Lisa...."

"Little is right."

"She doesn't deserve you."

"Come on, Mom."

"I want to go. I never had a high school prom. Instead we stood behind a bar while the boys brought out liquor to us. They got us drunk and fucked us in the alley next to the garbage cans. All I remember is coming home with a dress full of come and puke."

"Nice to know we still carry on the traditions of your youth, isn't it?"

"Take me."

She's going to start crying, I know it. She's been a mess since menopause. "Mom, I'm not taking you. I don't know where you got that dress...."

"At least you have to fuck me before you leave."

"Mom, really, it'll make me late."

"You have to!" she screams and starts crying. "Do it, you little piece of shit!"

"Yeah, if you say so, I guess." I put the gun into the holster and then put on the jacket to see how it looks. You can't really see the bulge, unless you're looking, of course. She's been fucking me since I was fourteen, when she caught me masturbating in her closet wearing her panty hose. We did it a lot for a while, but the idea of fucking her hasn't appealed to me much lately, since I started having sex with people my own age, but there's something just bizarre enough about her wearing the prom dress that my prick starts to stir. I turn around to face her.

"Fuck me, Johnny, fuck my dirty cunt. Fuck me for the last time."

"Okay, Mom."

I decide not to bother taking off any clothes. I unzip my fly and pull down my underpants and let my prick spring out. She turns her back on me and leans over the dresser, lifts up the skirt in the back, and shows me her cunt, then looks over her shoulder at me.

"Fuck me good, you little prick, make it count."

Her cunt is wet and hot as the inside of a casserole. As I stick it in, she starts moaning, "Oh god Johnny, I'm going to miss getting fucked by you so much. Swear you'll do it to me again sometime. I can't make you do it, not after tonight, but I want it, I want to be fucked by your beautiful prick. Please, there's nobody left to fuck after your father died, please do it to me."

"Why don't you just join a swinger's club, Mom?" I say. "Or get a dog. You could probably get a dog to fuck you. They don't care. Listen," I add, pulling out, "I have to fuck your asshole, your cunt isn't tight enough."

"Oh god no," she says, although this is our standard procedure. She's too uptight to ask to get fucked in the ass. There has to be some mitigating reason so she doesn't have to take responsibility.

She gets on her knees and sucks my dick to make it wetter, then crawls over to the bed and braces herself as I stick it in her asshole. She makes a retching sound. I guess it will be kind of lonely for her, but it's not my job to give her pleasure. I decide not to think about it.

Instead I think about Lisa and her slickness. Lisa's a little blond thing whose tits are small—most things about her are small—but her ass and mouth are big. She looks like such a good girl with her bleached hair, so "petite" just like the dress department at Macy's where she goes shoplifting with her pals. But when she opens her mouth, things change. Her lips part and it's like looking into the interior of a BMW, it's so soft and inviting in there, there's music playing, you just have to dive in. Yet there's nothing about her that cries "slut." You have to dig for it.

Normally she's fairly demure and retiring, despite her blond hair and nice figure and popular status at school, and it's this side of her that I like to top and humiliate. I like to embarrass her in the halls, make her "accidentally" expose herself to someone, or announce in a loud voice that I can smell her twat. The more it humiliates her, the more turned on I get. Once I made her stuff herself inside her locker wearing nothing but her cheerleader boots and skirt—no panties, no top. The only way she could get all the way in was by sticking her butt out into the hallway, where anybody could finger her or slap her ass cheeks or mark her up with ballpoint pens.

For a long time we just did things like that. But lately I've been finding out something else about my girlfriend. It's not the opposite of the shy, receptive, twinkie-like girl—it's simply a ravenous other that she becomes. This other side she calls Lizza. Sometimes she's Lisa for a whole date, or most of it, until the tenth or twentieth orgasm and Lizza starts to take control. Sometimes she's Lizza the whole night, running with me as we immolate ourselves and others. Sometimes she strobes between them, both totally out of control and totally in, completely my bitch and my sister at the same time.

"Ugh, oh god no." Mom is grunting and thrusting against me, smashing her clit against a pocket vibrator she brought with her. I really don't want my prick to get a lot of use this early in the night, but for old time's sake I fuck her until I come. "I'm coming now, Mom, you cunt," I gasp. It makes her cry.

I pull out and go to the bathroom and wash my dick, which is still sticking out through my fly. When I go by my room my mother is sitting on the floor crying, her prom dress all messed up, come leaking out of her asshole.

"I'll be here when you get back."

"Mom, it's over. I might not even come back."

"You promised."

"No, I didn't. I never promised shit. I gotta go, really."

"I'll kill myself."

"Oh, yeah?" I'm interested. "How?"

She's silent. After a while I figure she's just bluffing and turn to go. She gasps and tries to grab my ankles. I kick at her and, more by accident than anything else, hit her in the face. She subsides.

I leave her there sitting in a puddle of my come, grab the keys to the Ford, and leave. Really, it's a relief not to have to go through all that anymore. I hope she doesn't ask me.

I drive the few blocks over to Greg's house. The sun is getting low, reflecting off the green-gold lawns.

Greg, my best friend, was going to come with me and Lisa to the prom as a threesome, but at the last minute some girl called him and he ended up getting talked into taking her. She's actually some girl from another school, but for some reason she wanted to go to our prom and asked Greg. He finally said yes to this chick, who's named Cora, figuring that, if nothing else, she can be a victim.

I park on the side of his house and let myself in through the kitchen door, as I've been doing since the fifth grade. His house is a little bigger than ours; his father makes more money than mine did. The place seems deserted. I walk through the big family room, across the polyester long-wear carpet and over to the stairway, and go upstairs to his room.

His door has a big Patti Smith poster on it. I tap on it and open the door.

Inside Greg is sitting at a vanity table, wearing a robe, brushing his short wavy black hair.

"Who was it?" he asks.

"Who was what?"

"Who did you fuck? I can smell it on you."

"My mom."

He laughs.

"It was weird, she was wearing a prom dress, and she said she would be my date. It made me hard, but still...." I go sit on the bed under the Tiffany and Belinda Carlisle posters. "Are you still bringing that Cora thing?"

"Yeah, I have to go pick her up. What do you think, I should just go in this, huh?" Greg stands up and turns and lets the dressing gown fall from his shoulders. He's wearing nothing but a black leather merry widow that goes from his crotch to just above his nipples. It's hooked to stockings, and as I watch, he slips into a pair of patent leather high heels. The corset ends in a point just above his cunt hair; his dick is fully exposed.

I whistle. "Greggy, you look too good."

"Better than any prom dress, huh?"

"Way better. People will shit when they see you." I can feel desire starting up and roaring in me like a lawn mower.

"They'll do more than that."

He walks over to where I'm sitting until his cock is right in my face. I sink to my knees in front of him and mouth his penis. It gets hard between my lips as he runs his fingers through my hair.

"Are you going to do that now?" he asks coyly.

"Mm-hmm."

"Little slut," he says. "All I have to do is show it to you and you melt. What a little cunt you are. And don't you know it. If you were really a girl all the way through and not just a little boy slut, you'd be in such trouble."

"Remember the first time we did this?" I say, kissing the cockhead.

"Fuck, you're romantic," he laughs. "Yeah, I remember. Twelve years old. Didn't you think you'd found the best toy in the world?"

"It *is*."

He laughs and pushes me away. "Do it later."

"Not there," I say, swallowing my saliva. "Not at the prom. Let me do it now." My voice rasps with desire.

"Un-uh."

He goes over to the closet and gets out a black tuxedo. He puts on the jacket over the merry widow, no shirt and bow tie, just the leather and his collarbone and shoulders. Then he puts on the pants. He sees me watching. "Got to have something to get down *to*," he laughs.

Turning to the mirror, he says, "What about tonight? You've been there before, I haven't." He applies makeup.

Last year I went with a senior girl. "Yeah, well.... You know, it's like a prom. They have a big banquet room. You eat. You fuck around, and you go upstairs and play. We have a whole floor and there's a different kind of goodness in every room."

"What about the adults?"

"Supposed to be there, but they're never around. I think they're scared as shit."

"Tell me more."

I laugh, more like a bark. "It was kinda hairy because I was, you know, small fry, not a senior. It isn't just girls who get fucked up. Boys do too, especially if there's something about them, something that marks them as an outsider. It's like a scent you carry. The ones who belong smell enough like the pack to run with it; the outsiders can get in big trouble. Fortunately, I guess enough of Kali's pack-scent rubbed off on me."

"Plus your natural masterful personality made them not fuck with you."

"Plus," I agree. "The main thing is, I stayed out of the bad motherfuckers' way."

"Like tonight they're staying out of yours."

He's ready, turns around. I can't even bear to look at him without wanting him again. "And where you gonna be?" I ask.

"We'll find each other. Then we'll see how masterful you *aren't*."

I think if I stand there too long looking at him, I'll never go. I'll pull out my gun and make him stay with me. But tonight's the night, and besides, there's Lisa.

I go downstairs and get into the car and glide along the streets to Lisa's house. Through some weird developer's design, her house is exactly like Greg's, only in a mirror image. There are other ways Greg and Lisa are alike, too, besides having me as their boyfriend. They're both control queens who have to be taken a long way to give it up. They both like getting fucked in the ass. They both have missing teeth from where their fathers hit them.

As I ring her doorbell I'm exactly on time.

Her father opens the door. He's wearing a sweater and holding a pipe and looks just like that intensely square father in *MAD Magazine* cartoons. He's the president of some kind of big financial firm, and he's drunk, as always.

"Don't you look nice," he says, not moving aside to let me in.

"Good evening, Mr. Money. Is Lisa ready yet?"

He just stands there looking hostile. I wait patiently. After eighteen years, I can wait another few minutes.

"Can I come in?"

"Lisa's grounded."

"Oh really?"

"You'll never see her alive again," he announces.

Finally his wife comes up behind him and says, "For goodness sake, Herb, let the poor boy in."

He snickers, lets her take him back through the foyer into the living room. I follow them and sit on the couch as he collapses into his chair and stares at me. He lights his pipe. After a few minutes of silence, he says, "Drive carefully," and then giggles, because he knows that driving is the least of Lisa's worries.

She comes downstairs all perfect, the hair piled up on her head in that ridiculous prom hairstyle that girls still go for. She's dressed to match me in an oatmeal-colored dress with full petticoats. It's not just a prom dress, it's a homecoming queen's dress. Like Greg's corset, it's strapless, stopping just above her nipples. You can see all of the black widow tattoo between her tits.

"Hi, Johnny," she says. She has a look on her face like she's in a trance. In fact, she is. Most of the girls put themselves into a trance state that lasts for hours to get through events like the prom. It's one of the improvements since my mother's youth. Her forehead glistens and she breathes with her mouth open, licking her lips.

Lisa sits down in an armchair. She balances on her crinolines. We're really doing this prom up right.

"How are you doing in school, John?" asks her Dad, wheezing.

Her mother appears with a camera. "Pictures!" she exclaims brightly. It's something to do to keep from talking to one another.

We rise and she takes pictures of us. I realize she's crying.

Finally we get ready to go. We go into the foyer. Her father says, "Before you go, don't you remember what you promised?"

As we, the other male and I, watch, her mother, who is also wearing a prom dress, leans against the wall and lifts her skirts. Lisa gets on her knees and leans forward and begins to suck her cunt. While she's getting eaten, the woman screams at her husband, "Herb! You piece of shit! You never fucked me like this. You never gave me this much pleasure. That's why me and little Lisa go to bed together every time we can, every time you're gone, because you're such a piece of shit and you never fuck me, all you do is sit like that smoking your pipe and driving me into the arms of perversity, you shit, you shit, you shit, you shit," and then she comes.

They stay that way for a while: Mom leaning up against the wall, the skirt sagging out of her hand; Lisa buried between her legs; her father watching everything and smiling. I'm waiting for something else to happen. There's nothing strange about all this. People fuck each other all the time. That's not what tonight is about, though. Tonight is about degradation.

The husband stirs. "The last part," he croaks. He goes over to Lisa and pulls her away from his wife's cunt.

"Little girl," her father says, taking her chin in his hand, rubbing it between his fingers to feel the moistness that dribbled there. "Don't forget that, tonight of all nights, you have to do what the boys want."

"And the girls!" her mother moans, her fingers deep in her snatch.

Her father slaps his wife as hard as he can. She flies across the room. I think he's going to fling himself on his daughter now and I'm waiting for it to happen but it doesn't; Lisa just sits there and waits on her knees, timing her breathing until it's right again.

Her mother comes back and fits her cunt to her daughter's mouth and howls as she opens her bladder. When I look at the father, drool is coming out of his mouth. Piss splashes across Lisa's mouth, across her tits, all down her perfect prom costume. The dress soaks up an enormous amount of piss on its own but can't stop the little rivulets from running between her tits over the open field above the neckline of her dress.

I feel like I'd like to kill somebody right now. Maybe the man will kill his wife and I won't have to. But after she pisses she sinks to her knees just like my mother did, sinks to her knees in a puddle while we go out the door.

While we're walking to the car I tell Lisa, "That's how you'll end up."

"If you're good to me," she replies.

We get into the car and I start it. She sits there passively. We drive down the suburban tree-lined streets, down bigger and bigger boulevards like little streams joining into a big river. Through and out of the ugly suburb and onto the freeway toward the city.

Driving on the freeway, I look over at her. Her hair is already fucked up, and her dress is covered with urine. Her window is open to let it air out a little. She's sitting there sort of vacantly, sitting there in the place she has to be in to get through this night unless somebody kills her first.

It could happen. The last prom ended with six girls sailing off the roof of the Hyatt Regency, thirty-two stories into the street below like so many smashed cocktail glasses. Nobody knows whether they were pushed or whether one jumped on purpose and the others followed, intoxicated, their hands between their legs all the way down and shrieking shrieking.

I know that one.

"Raise your dress over your knees, Lisa bitch," I say. She does, slowly.

"Higher higher higher," I say by turns. "That's the way. Just sit there and show me your steaming cunt. Now explain our relationship."

"You're my boyfriend," she says. "No matter what you do to me, no matter what everyone else does to me, you're my boyfriend. That means you'll stay with me and protect me. You won't let me get thrown off the roof like those girls last year. You won't let me get strangled or drowned in a toilet or shot up and overdosed with too much shit. Not unless you do it yourself. Only when you kill me can I find my destiny. I know you'll protect me until then."

"Urinate."

The piss streams out of her.

2

We arrive at the big hotel and get out. A little monkey-like valet takes my keys and disappears to use my car for drug smuggling for the rest of the night. If he's quick he can get to Laredo and back by checkout time.

Lisa is totally piss-stained. But as we stand in the gleaming entryway of the huge hotel, it's obvious other people are in worse shape. Cars pull up with couples, threesomes, and quartets. Most of the girls are already disheveled. One girl's pink prom dress is already little more than rags; underneath there's a lot of complicated underwear, some of it cut open with a knife and hanging loose, some of it still in the place it was meant to be, approximately. She has a big black eye she didn't get on the ride into town; judging by that, and her ecstatic expression, she must be in the middle of a scene that's already lasted more than a day.

A car pulls up and two guys and a girl get out, and the girl is holding an extra prom dress over her arm; one of the guys opens the back door of the car and out crawls a girl I recognize as one of the big principal's assistants in the office. Usually she's Little Miss Prim and Proper and never lets anybody use the copier. Now she's butt naked except for a collar and a leash and a butt plug that has a horse tail attached to it. She crawls across the greasy driveway on her hands and knees, muttering, "Ouch, this concrete is fucking hot."

They've all been fucked by at least one parent before they've been allowed to come here. Just so they won't forget where they came from. But the parents also know that that's the last time, unless the kid wants some more. That's what Prom Night is all about, and that's why all the parents take pictures and cry.

Now it's our turn. This time we win.

A limousine pulls up to the curb and the door opens and seventeen naked people spill out. They just keep coming, I can't believe there's so many. They're already covered with lube and shit and come and piss. They've been in the limo for less than an hour, and they're all high on LSD.

There are four het couples, four gay male couples, and four dyke couples. And someone's slave.

All the bottoms line up on the curb after the limo pulls away. They all get on their knees. Some of the bottoms are women and some are men. It doesn't matter. Their tops all scream in unison, NOW! And piss runs out of all the kids lined up on the curb. It makes me hot, it makes me want to make Lisa do it again for me. But I wait a second. I can see the slave. She's seventeen and her red hair is to die for.

She's wrapped around a boy and never stops licking him, never stops touching him and whispering to him. Unless there's something more important for her to do. But she doesn't join in the line at the curb. She wraps around her boy and tongue-fucks him in the mouth while all the urine is running down the pavement. It sparkles in the late-setting sun.

A van pulls up behind the limo and a delivery man rolls out a clothing rack. It's the clothes of all the naked kids from the limo. Their garments, all perfect prom dresses and tuxes, are still pristine. We have to save something.

"Let's get into some air conditioning!"

We stream inside, up to the ballroom. The room is big enough to house the space shuttle. The walls are so distant they're indistinct. Countless round banquet tables of kids. All dressed up and this place to go.

Lots of messed-up hair. But we buck up. Pretending to be adults, we put on a good face, try to do it straight for a while. Dinner is served: roast beef and mashed potatoes.

I'm vaguely aware that high schools used to have proms in the gym. I guess I've gotten that from movies. But at some point, the instinct of high school students to imitate rich adults in every aspect of their lives broke through and some bright kid realized that adults don't have dances in gymnasiums, they have banquets in huge hotels. So now we have to.

That's okay. It makes it easier to get to your hotel room afterward. And you don't have to worry about messing up the gym floor, snicker snicker.

We eat. People are actually worried about which fork to use on which course. They're not just pretending, they're actually concerned about doing it right. I can't decide whether that makes me sick or not. It's nice to follow the form, but you start to wonder about people who don't show the proper irony, who don't indicate they realize the form is just a framework on which to hang our transgressions. It just makes me anxious for the transgressions to begin.

People at the next table are getting drunk. They've been getting drunk all day. Some people are into that kind of degradation. They hang out together. Later they'll go upstairs to the drinker's hallway. I've never been into it. When I want to get high, I take something. Some guy bursts out laughing in that disgusting way drunk people have that sounds like puking: *Ur-hur-huuurrrrghhh-haw.*

Onstage there are a few exhibits. The girl who got pregnant, of course she's there, prom dress, her belly full, sitting shackled to a chair. Every year one girl is chosen to be the one who gets pregnant; she's irreverently known as the "Mother of the Year." She gets fucked in September so that, by Prom Night, she's ready to give birth. Before she leaves she takes something to induce labor, and then does it, right there onstage.

There's also some apparatus to keep people enchained, etc., and a big cage like the kind they put Russian mass murderers in when they're in court. I saw it on TV.

Nothing happens until one of the girls gets beneath the table and starts sucking off men and women indiscriminately. She reaches me and opens my pants. It's times like this I wish I was one of the guys wearing skirts. There are some, naturally. She takes out my cock and rubs it up against her face. It's still slightly sticky from my mother's snatch, but this girl, whoever she is, she doesn't care, she's there to please. She swallows my prick as her boyfriend looks into my eyes and says, "If ever once you feel her teeth, cut her fucking throat instantly."

It's a great incentive for her, and she makes me come without touching me with her teeth. Nevertheless, later that night I see her with her throat cut. I only hope it was her own boyfriend who did it to her. I guess if he ordered it, it was the same thing.

Now I'm Lizza for a while. I really like this dirty story. I worship my boyfriend's fat prick and I like it most when he gives it to me in the ass. My favorite fuck was at Spring Break when he was fucking me from behind so hard that he busted the window with my head and drove me through it, and draped me over the broken windowsill still fucking me, screaming and screaming, until he came, the sperm mixing with my blood. That was hot for me because I was high on LSD and speed. It's hot for me to see my own blood.

I'm lucky. I belong to the sorority of nine. Not nine girls—nine months, one for each month of the school year. At the beginning of the year we time our cycles until they're all the same, until we're all ready to start bleeding on Prom Night. Then maybe if our boyfriends fuck our bloody cunts they won't have to kill us just to see it. We're trying to train them to cut us safely, but then there are always motherfuckers (ha ha ha) who get carried away, and always somebody dies. In fact, twenty or thirty people die at each prom. The whole point of the sorority of nine, which is so secret it doesn't even have a name, is to prepare us to survive the prom.

But it's not just a torture evening. It's fun for me too. Sex gets me off. I dig the taste of sperm. I like it when it's got a little bit of shit mixed in with it, that means the boy has just been fucking me or somebody else in the ass. I like it best when it's a faggot who's been fucking another faggot in the ass and then I get to lick their shit-smeared penises.

I have two goals: to get through this alive and to please my boyfriend. I want to please him because I love him, but it's deeper than that. I was linked to him even before I was born. Secretly, he's my brother.

My brother, I mean my boyfriend, loves me so much. He treats me fairly well, considering.

We're sitting next to each other while some cunt is sucking him off. "Tell me," *he says, gasping slightly,* "what your father does to you."

"He hits me," *I whisper in his ear.*

"Don't whisper it, you cunt, speak it out loud."

"My father hits me. He breaks his hand across my face. I dig it. I beg him to. The times I like best are when I can both feel and hear the bones in my face cracking—do it, do it, do it, Daddy, hit me, hit me." *I say this to make him come in the whore's mouth—that's a laugh. As if they had to pay anybody to do this.*

That's true, what I said about my father. It's only true in my mind. It's what I wanted him to do. I wanted him to break my face, then maybe it would be what he likes. He doesn't like me.

I need to transfer my need for Daddy to my boyfriend. He's the one protecting me now. Maybe if I'm really nice he'll kill my parents for me. I want to see them die while he fucks them in the ass with hot pokers, their tongues melting as they reach for each other in ecstasy, I want to see their blood spill across the floor.

I don't want to have to clean it up. I hate fucking cleaning up. That's why we have the prom in a big hotel.

He comes in the whore's mouth. I skip under the table and kiss her and get his sperm. I surface again and tell him, "It's okay, I got your come in my mouth. I got some of it." I promised him to always go where his come goes. If he fucks someone in the ass, I have to suck his come out of their ass. If he comes in someone's mouth, I have to kiss them and get it. If he comes on the floor I have to lick it up. I'm a dog who has to fetch his come when he throws it. I'll wade into anything to please him.

He likes seeing me like this: on my knees, really disheveled, piss-stained, his come dribbling out of my mouth. That's a pretty picture for him.

If I please him, he won't kill me. I'll last.

After a while the food starts streaking through the air. The main point is to keep it out of your hair. A little corn gets in my hair, but that's all right, corn is like shit. Anything that's like shit is okay.

The whole banquet rises like a wave, and after the wave has crested the food is just everywhere in the air. It's flying like hail, I can't believe there could be so much. It's an incredible amount of food flying through the air: roast beef with a LOT of gravy. Mashed potatoes. Peas, those disgusting canned ones. And corn, lots of it. I envision banks of little chippers in the kitchen, chittering the corn off those corncobs with their teeth.

Corn muffins.

I slip under the table again to get out of the fray. There's a girl across the table, and I push through the legs to get to her, then shove my mouth under her dress. I fasten across her cunt like a leech and start sucking. Ugh ugh ugh, her period comes. This is a problem for her, because it's supposed to be for her boyfriend. But she lowers her head just enough for me to hear, "Lisa, I've been in love with you for years and now you're finally sucking my cunt like I've yearned for. Suck my fucking bloody cunt, it's you that it's for, it's not for my boyfriend. I love you."

When Lisa comes up from underneath the table, blood is streaked across her face and down her chest. I can't believe there's so much.

"That was groovy," she says. "She just pissed out blood. Sorry Frank," she says to the girl's boyfriend, and then we all laugh really loudly at the guy, everyone knows he's a faggot anyway and the only reason he has a girl is because it's, like, just so important to his parents.

Frank laughs too, we're laughing with him, not at him. The whole stupid idea of going with a girl to the prom just because your parents are so stupid they can't see you're a faggot—plus, because he internalized it for so long, he was in the closet until just earlier this year.

He had to come out before he got killed. It's only the closeted fags who get shit at our school. If there's one thing we can't stand, it's hypocrisy.

The room, which was fairly calm ten minutes ago, before the food fight, is in an uproar. People are walking and running around, some of them rolling in the mess that's on the floor. I hear furniture splitting. Up on the stage, the girl who's tied to the chair, the pregnant girl, is moaning. People gather round. But it's nothing, it's just a bowel movement. We watch as it splatters out of her. Then everyone turns away to resume their business.

In the cage near the Mother of the Year, people are getting imprisoned. It's like a coat check, only it's for people. You put your girl-friend or boyfriend in there so they won't run off and get killed while you're involved in something else. Of course, the imprisoned people roam the cage itself, made of iron bars, and once you're inside, you really can't escape until your lover comes back for you.

Lisa takes my hand and leads me up to the lip of the stage, and we look up into the cage. Right now, for some reason, most of the people in it are guys. I recognize several basketball players. Our school is so huge you don't really know someone unless they're in one of your classes, you just see them at pep rallies and assemblies. I spot some guy I vaguely recognize; he's holding on to the bars of the cage, bracing himself, getting fucked standing up by one of the basketball players. The basketballer is so tall he has to bend his knees to reach the normal-sized guy's ass.

"If I was a guy, then getting fucked in the ass would be so dirty," Lisa says. "It would be the only place where I could get fucked, and I'd be real tight and you'd have to do it to me. You'd be my older brother fucking me and taking advantage of me and teaching me how to punk."

Lisa has this ridiculous idea that I'm her brother. All right, if it turns her on, sure. But we're aren't. Really. I wish we were. I wish we were brother and sister and could be like Bonnie and Clyde and kill everyone. But we aren't related.

We wander back through the ballroom. There are still some people sitting at tables eating dessert who look pretty pissed off, they're so alienated, so out of touch with their bodies, that they don't even know how to stand up and take part in the orgy. Eventually they'll get up and wander out of the hotel and get in their cars and wonder what to do. I used to be like that, unable to join in, terrified of other people. It's just self-hatred. Once I learned that everybody else was just as bad as me, I got over it.

Back at our table, there's a guy spasming and convulsing while he comes into the mouth of the girl who is still making her way around the table sucking everyone off. He stops jerking after a while. For a minute I think somebody might have poisoned him. But it's just the way he comes.

I hope I do/I hope I don't look like that. I want to lose it without losing it. I want to be degraded as much as I want to degrade, but it's risky to reveal your need for it and have it happen safely, and so forth. It's much faster just to do it to somebody else.

"Lisa," I say, "be my girlfriend and fuck someone."

"Anyone...Who? Him?" she asks, motioning to a passing boy.

"No...fuck *him*," I say, pointing at some drunk. Lisa leans back over an adjacent table and lifts up her skirts and says "Fuck my cunt, lucky boy!" He fucks her. I watch her get it. After watching from behind I walk around the table so I can watch her face. It's still blood-streaked from her secret admirer, who is even now humiliating her so-called boyfriend and making plans to go off with my Lisa on a fun-filled forever to Mexico.

A trip down there to fuck. You pick up a whore and take her to another town. You fuck her in full view of everyone. Then you sell her meat. Then you can kill her while fucking her one last time, then her body is cut up and the meat is taken away by the buyers.

Secretly Lisa was a Mexican whore in another lifetime, it was revealed to her. Her body was cut up...maybe it's the beef that's flying through the air still. Lisa's quest through eternity is to collect and ingest the dispersed parts of her original whore body. When she shits out the very last part of her old body, that's when she can enter into heaven.

A girl comes up to me. She's one of the dykes in our class. I respect her limits. We both watch my girlfriend get fucked while the dyke states she could do better with her hand. The guy takes a long time, who does he think he is? I am suddenly enraged. I take out the revolver from my shoulder holster and fire a bullet through the brain of the guy fucking my girlfriend.

"Oh god, he's coming like that," Lisa croaks as the fucked-up, brains-splattered guy jerks his last load into her. "God, what a feeling. Oh Johnny, do it again."

All the guys at the table suddenly remember other appointments. The dyke laughs.

"Come on, slut," I growl at Lisa and drag her across the floor. The floor of the ballroom is thick with food and debris—smashed furniture, pieces of clothing. Blood runs in streaks through the wreckage; in other places, it's thick with white wine.

I drag her across the floor toward the stage. The chick in the chair is giving birth.

I have to be true. I run with all the girls across the floor and circle up around the chick while one girl catches the baby as it comes spilling out. The baby is lifted off to safety, and we all run to smear our faces in the girl's bloody cunt.

This is a crucial time. Usually the birth-giving girl at the prom then dies by her boyfriend's hand in a shower of blood. But this girl's a dyke and she's got a dyke girlfriend. It's intense.

The girlfriend towers above her, protecting her. She's at least seven feet tall, and not at all elongated, just a big girl—she was all-state in basketball. Then she bleats and her period starts, she doesn't have her skirts lifted up and so you get to watch the blood slowly seep out through the layers of prom dress cloth. She'd die to protect her girlfriend. But we're here too.

"Fuck this dyke shit!" screams a guy.

Johnny blows his brains out and people fall on him with their table knives, cut him up into a million pieces, and eat them. I manage to get almost his entire dick, and giggle as I stuff it up my butt temporarily.

"You should have waited until he was fucking me."

The girl who gave birth now gives the afterbirth. Lizza rolls in the blood with twenty other chicks. Somehow, when all the chicks emerge from this, their dresses, where still intact, are only streaked, not soaked, in blood.

I pull her over to the side a little and lean back against the wall. The more blood I see, the more turned on I get. Lizza gets on her knees and sucks me as I watch another couple. A boy leads a pretty girl with platinum blond hair to the wall of the room. He kisses her and rubs his body up against hers. When she's totally turned on, he plunges a knife into her again and again while she screams. I buck back and forth in Lizza's mouth.

I look down at Lisa, disheveled, blood-streaked, come dribbling out of her mouth. "I love you," she says. "I know you love me enough to at least get me as turned on as that chick was before you murder me."

"At least she got to die in front of other people," I say.

"Yeah, everybody gets their fifteen minutes, right?"

At this moment the seventeen people on LSD enter the room for the first time. They've been upstairs and they're cleaned off and dressed perfectly. There isn't a single stain on them.

The room quiets down and watches them. It's almost a reverent feeling. They form a procession and parade around the room. The only stain on them is where their trains drag in the debris.

Then you can see them getting turned on. They all stop where they are, sway slightly, turn outwards, and begin urinating in their clothing.

If anybody at the prom had held back up to now, this was when they lost it. A huge cheer rises up as the wet stains crop up and spread through the clothes of the acid queens. As the puddles start forming on the floor around their legs, I look around to see people fastening their mouths to others' mouths, to pricks, to cunts. They're falling on the floor and coupling, tripling, quadrupling. A guy reaches for me, and I start to push him away, but then his fist slams me upside the head and he says, "You don't *get* away from me, motherfucker."

It's Greg. The jacket and pants he'd been wearing are gone, but he's still in his leather merry widow, tits still being pushed up firmly, and although his hair is soaked and matted with various substances, the way he's wearing that leather thing just makes me want to lick him clean. The sight of my own boyfriend, after being someone else's boyfriend all evening long, is such a relief that I almost collapse.

He catches me by the hair and pushes me down to my knees. Lizza is there behind me. She lifts up Greg's prick, stuffs it in my mouth, and then standing behind me, shoves my head forward with her crotch.

They sandwich me between them, kissing, shoving their crotches together, only I'm in between. I'm ecstatic. Lisa and Greg don't really know each other, despite the fact that they've been sharing me for the last seven or eight months, and I've always wondered what would happen when they got together. Now I know: I get turned into lube between them.

Greg's prick swells in my mouth and turns into a battering ram. I don't need to remember the things that turn him on and make fucking my mouth good for him because I've been going down on him for years, getting fucked in the mouth while he laughs and gasps and tears me apart. Greg's prick fills my mouth perfectly because I've grown up sucking it, my mouth grew to be the perfect shape for his prick to fuck.

Johnny's head, smashed between my cunt and Greg's, is bony as I fuck against it, my skirts lifted, my naked cunt rubbing against the hair on his head that's just long enough to grab. I wrap my arm around Greg's shoulders and pull his mouth to mine, and it's like there isn't enough for us to bite or lick. I feel like I'm on acid myself, only I'm not. I'm just here in Lisa's body in the middle of a horrendously great fucking scene.

Greg is making noises in my mouth and I realize he's about to come, so I swallow his tongue and dig my nails into his neck, the hair trailing deliriously wet past my fingers. From on the other side of Johnny's head, I feel him pump into Johnny's mouth, and I shove forward, giving resistance where Johnny, that slut, has none.

Greg takes his mouth away from mine and throws his head back and I throw my head back and we scream together just like the Klingon death yell. Johnny falls away. I reach forward and stuff Greg's just-come prick into me for as long as it stays hard, but I can't quite get off.

"I need fucking," I gasp. Greg looks at Johnny, who's no good, he's just struggling to his feet. Johnny has a role problem: Catch him right and he disappears. I don't have that problem as Lisa/Lizza, I'm either one or the other, always taking it, but always somebody. Johnny wants too much to disappear. It would worry me, but tonight, only the strong survive.

"Knock some sense into him or he won't last long," I advise Greg. "You're his boyfriend, take care of him, or kill him and take me." I stumble over to the acid queens, to some guy dressed in a blood-colored tux. I dig through my skirts, which are really getting to be a drag—lots of chicks have gone to plan B, which is dump the prom dress and go with the fetching rip-me-to-shreds lingerie underneath. I come up with my cunt and present to him, "Give me your dick," I say. He clearly isn't sure what is happening, so I plunge my hand deep inside my pussy and come up with some fresh juice, which I smear across his face. "Fuck me, capeesh?" I insist. His body understands, even if his mind is elsewhere; I see his prick rising in his piss-stained trousers.

I can't wait for this guy to figure out his own zipper, much less make it through my petticoats. I swing my leg out behind his knees and knock him down, then rip frantically at his pants. He still has a belt on, and I wrap it around my hand and wrist for later use. If I had a knife, I'd cut his fucking pants away, but I don't, so I laboriously pull them down to his knees as he lies helpless on his back, and finally finally jam his prick home into my cunt.

I ride his body, the skirts helping me to balance. Someone's walking toward me, it's Greg and Johnny. Or rather Greg dragging Johnny. Surrounded by my dress, I can't show them my cunt plunging up and down on the boy's dick, but I choke out, "I'm getting fucked, I'm getting fucked"— put in the passive tense to try to bring Johnny back to me. "I'm getting fucked but you're my boyfriend. You can do anything to me. I still have your come on my face, you just raped my mouth ten minutes ago. Johnny, I need it from you, I'm your bitch, I'm your bitch."

"See?" Greg says. "That's what I saved you for." He kisses Johnny and then slaps him hard, like in that commercial. Johnny shakes his head like a dog, and then he's okay again.

"Tell me," I beg him.

"Lizza," he says, "you're my sister." He squats down next to me and reaches for my clit, and as soon as he touches it, I start coming on the prick that I'm riding. My skirts are so full that there's no question of him holding me from behind and diddling me, he just has to hang on from the side as I come on the fat prick of some drug-addled teenager.

I spin away from Lizza when she finishes coming and see one of the acid-doped chicks, she's leaning up against the wall and masturbating. I recognize her from my English class last year, she was the artsy type who insisted on reading Lady Macbeth's part. Long-straight-black-haired girl, standing and masturbating in front of people because she's on acid. She doesn't focus on me as I come up to her. With one hand I push her head back by the throat, with the other I jam three fingers into her sopping cunt. Another girl comes up and kisses this chick, I realize they're some of the dykes from that limo. They suck each other's faces and then the girlfriend says, "Fuck her good, baby, she desires it."

That just makes my dick hard so I pull it out of my pants—god, how I wish I had a dress on instead of this put-it-back-in, take-it-back-out shit—and cram it into Lady Macbeth as her girlfriend laughs. When I look to the side I see Greg and Lizza kissing, then Lizza sees me looking and flashes me a peace sign.

My come feels really good squirting into the dyke's cunt.

3

Lizza drags me into the hallway outside the ballroom. Let's see, how many have died so far? Three that I know of, but two of them, I shot personally. I remember that she asked for some of that again. I grab some guy, he must be from another school, I don't recognize him, I say, Come here and fuck my girlfriend's pus*sy*. I grab him by the hair and drag his face over to her cunt like he's a dog who has to scent to get the idea. She leans back over a table next to the ballroom door, a table sitting there for people to hand out nametags or something. His prick bursts out of his pants as he straightens up and sinks it in Lizza's cunt.

"Make it last," she wails. The guy thinks she's talking to him. "Oh, yes, baby. Oh, yes, baby."

She can see me take the gun out.

"Oh, yes, take me closer," she begs. "Not yet. Not yet. Let him get close. Oh, you motherfucker, fuck my fucking cunt. Fuck me, you pig."

I pull the hammer back and put it next to the guy's temple.

"Fuck me fuck me fuck me, now, Johnny, now, he's squirting, oh Johnny, do it, do it, ah gawd I'm coming" and I let her come on his prick until right in the middle of the very last moment of his orgasm I sink the bullet into his head.

Lizza screams filth, *fuck fuck fcukfuckcckfuckucfkucfkuck*. She wants to fly apart. She finds his mouth and sinks her teeth into his lips, biting them off. He's dead anyway. His body flops.

We leave him there in the hall. A hundred people watched the show and applaud. A girl yells at me, "Hey, come here and kill my boyfriend, too."

Greg has followed us out of the ballroom. He looks so good in his getup, but now I keep hold of myself so I won't melt again. "You guys come up to the seventh floor. There's lots of shit happening."

"Like what?" I say, already bored. I want to fuck him.

Greg says, "Well, one room is the naked room. It's just one big cluster fuck. No weapons allowed—I guess you could strangle somebody if you could get a grip. Of course, to get there you have to get past everything else."

"Wait, tell me in a second. Lisa, suck me." She gets on her knees, insatiable.

"People are shooting up in one room," Greg says. "In another room, the girls are tied to a table and they're getting fucked over and over, they're a mess of sperm. They don't even have hairstyles left.

"In another room, girls are doing it to each other. They're fisting each other.

"In another room, there's a girl chained to a post, and people, guys and girls, are whipping her. She's saying really cool things, like she can't decide if she loves it, if she wants to die, if she wants them to stop or not. If you get there in time, you can see the blood start running down her legs.

"In another room, people are smoking crack and killing one another and fucking one another. In fact that's a whole wing, that's the let's-fuck-up wing.

"In another room is where chicks go to get pissed on—either their boyfriends tell them to or they want it."

"Bingo," I say. "What's the number of that room?"

"717."

I grab Lisa and pull her to her feet. "This is where it gets serious, baby sister," I say. Her eyes widen because I called her that. Anything for effect.

I put a leather collar on her. We get into an elevator. There are these glass elevators ascending and descending in the lobby, and it's like a joke to put on a show for people in the lobby. All the people who get drunk are down there watching people fuck while they go up and down. Some asshole in the lobby is taking target practice at the elevators as they go by, like it's a shooting range, but he's such a lousy shot that he can't hit a fucking thing. The shots ring down off the walls like bells until finally somebody's been hit in the foot by a ricochet. That just makes everybody laugh harder.

Our elevator contains three prom couples and one straight couple. The straight couple are thinking, Oh shit, I totally forgot what it's like on prom weekends.

They're so old they never fuck. All the fucking all around them hardly sinks in. They just want to go home. They don't want to let it sink in.

One of the prom couples is fucking his girlfriend in the elevator while she wraps her legs around him. She has really great legs and is like a fucking model, she is perfect as she wraps herself around and gets fucked and laid open by her boyfriend.

We arrive at the seventh floor. The elderly couple doesn't get out; the husband is holding his finger over the DOOR CLOSE button, and he starts jamming on it as we step out.

In the hallway, of course, are people making out, people jacking themselves and each other off, pouring alcohol all over, etc., etc.—typical teenage behavior. Nobody is so gross as to actually have intercourse in the hallway. There are so many rooms for that.

I take Lisa down to 717 and open the door. There are no beds in there, it's just an empty room with a lamp on the floor, lying on its side, but still on, the only light in the room. There are fourteen chicks on the floor on their knees. Boys and girls push past me into the room and piss on these chicks. A few of them look like they're on something.

I push Lisa down to her knees and say, "Stay here until I come to get you. When I come to get you I might just kill you. But stay here until then."

Now I'm Lisa. Down on my knees, I'm begging you please. What am I begging. It doesn't matter. A girl comes up to me and pulls my face into her cunt as she pisses. I like it and it turns me on that my brother wants me to be here getting degraded just as much as anybody else's girlfriend.

The girl who pissed on me leaves without a word. I look as the girl next to me gets a faceful. She's pretty. Oh, I know her, she used to be in my sophomore math class. She catches me looking at her. "Does this turn you on as much as it does me?" she asks.

"The only thing better would be if you fisted me while I get pissed on,"
I reply. She raises her urine-soaked hand and I bend over. It's inside me like an alien, fucking me. A guy comes and pisses in my face. Oh god this is low.

I follow Greg down the hall. We enter a room where somebody holds my face up to a long line of coke. I inhale it and my cock gets instantly hard. Some girl jams her pussy on my prick and takes me for a ride. She comes and shoots, and then turns around—it's actually a boy, I've been fucking his ass, I bend down and suck off his long, long prick. Somebody gives me more coke. I penetrate the boy's asshole again. I hold him down. This boy is so pretty in his prom dress. Too bad I didn't come like that.

We stagger into another room. It's kind of an indistinct room. There's a guy barfing over in the corner and people's coats are on the bed. I guess people just come here to catch their breath.

I drag Greg into the bathroom. Somehow he knows what I want. We fall to our knees kissing each other, our mouths digging for each other's cocks. Lisa is getting pissed on while I'm in here sucking some guy's cock. I dig it.

I sprawl on the floor, leaning half up against the bathtub, and let Greg cut my pants off with a knife. Then he lowers his mouth onto my cock and tickles my balls. "You bitch," I whisper, mostly to turn myself on.

A girl comes and stands in the doorway and watches us, impassive. Dressed only in souvenir panties with the word BURNS printed across the butt, she doesn't look familiar, and she doesn't seem to be with anybody. "His mouth's on my prick," I tell her. "Too bad you don't know what it's like to have a prick and get sucked off by a pretty boy.... When I think about what we've done together, how much pleasure we've had, how many people we've fucked, I get dizzy. Too bad you don't have a prick to fuck his ass with while he sucks me."

She smiles slightly. "Too bad you don't have a cunt you could catch more boys with," she retorts. "That's all you want, isn't it, you faggot? That's what you are, aren't you? Even though it's you getting your cock sucked, in reality you're the punk. You like to get fucked as much as you like to fuck. Even more, when it's your boyfriend here."

"Yes," I breathe. She's turning me on.

"In the middle of this whole orgy, you two come in here to be alone. You're so selfish. And where do you pick? A toilet! Typical of little queers who like to suck each other's cocks."

"Oh, god," I say, my eyes rolling back. As much as I like to call Lisa cunt, whore, bitch, slut, I like to get called queer when I'm doing it in some nasty way, like with a boy. And she can tell.

"Little faggot, little queer, little bitch. You're so helpless like that. You're so helpless, fag."

With a shout I come into Greg's mouth. "Oh jesus."

"That's right, queer, come in his mouth." When I look at her, she's smiling and rubbing herself through her panties, but when I look back, she's gone.

Greg comes up for air. "Who was that?" he asks.

"I don't know, some girl."

He wipes his mouth. "Turn around."

I get on my knees on the hard tile floor of the bathroom. He unwraps a little bar of soap and foams up his hands, then gets his prick slick. While he fucks me we talk about ways to humiliate our girlfriends more.

"Let's cut all their hair off."

"Let's kill somebody and make them eat their genitals."

"I really like it when Lizza's face is all bloody."

"I'd love to see Cora's face covered with blood."

"I guess the best most ultimate thing we could do is kill them right here while we fuck them."

"Then we'd have to kill each other while we shoot off into each other's mouths."

"God, then where would we be."

"I don't know, it has a certain appeal."

"It's all the backwards-masked rock music you listen to that makes you want to kill yourself, but I'll save you from that," I promise Greg. I want his lips badly. In the room I can hear somebody getting whipped over and over again with a belt, the slapping sound alternating with moans and yelps of increasing intensity. Greg is driving his cock in and out, looking for something to make him come.

"What's the difference between someone you fuck and kill, and someone you just fuck?" I wonder.

"How should I know, you're the one that's been doing all the killing."

"Yeah, but not really before tonight."

"Don't theorize," he growls. "If you're going to talk about it, do it in a way that'll make me come."

"All right. Where's your fucking date? Where's Cora?"

"She's a wet blanket," he said. "She's from another school,

right? You know who she actually is? She's my cousin."

"I can't believe you had to take your cousin to the prom. Okay, let's kill her."

"Tell me, make me come."

"We'll take her upstairs at the end of the night. We'll be some of the first people on the roof. There's a railing up there that goes around the edge; we can handcuff her to that and fuck her and cut her."

"Ugh, tell me," he groans.

"Just that: You'll be fucking Lisa, who'll be lying on the ground, right beneath Cora, and I'll stand up and fuck Cora. Then when I come I'll cut her and you can see the blood squirt through the air. It would get Lisa off, that's for sure."

"Tell me," he insists.

"But the best part is that we'll make her want it.... We'll make her beg to get fucked, we'll make her beg to get cut.... Can't you hear her voice now, asking for it while we do it to her?"

Greg gasps and rams deep into my ass and comes, yelling.

"I'll let you hold her legs," I add.

He yells louder, pushes harder. "That cunt!" he gasps. "God, that would be good." He twists, seeking sensation for his exploding cock. "Fuck, fuck, fuck," he whispers. Then finally he's still.

"Okay," Greg says.

He pulls out of me and when I turn around to sit, I can see the same girl standing in the doorway watching us. She is now entirely naked, her short brown hair more fucked up. Her eyes glow, either from watching us or from the coke that people are doing in that other room.

"I just got fucked," she announces. "But I guess you guys can't get it up for a girl, can you? What a couple of useless fucks."

"God, you're hostile, what's your problem?"

"She's high," Greg tells me.

"Why don't we go ask my girlfriend," I continue, "whether or not we can get it up, since she's gotten fucked by both of us tonight."

She raises an eyebrow. Greg and I each take an arm and hurry her out into the hallway. Sperm is dripping out of my ass, and all I'm wearing now is a shirt and my oatmeal-colored tux jacket. I feel kind of exposed.

"Just a second," I tell Greg. He holds the naked girl, who is starting to struggle, and I stop a girl going by who looks about my size. She's stumbling, really zonked on something. "Excuse me," I say, putting my hand gently around her throat, "you have something I need."

She just sighs and says, "Just do it in my cunt. Do it in my cunt. My ass has had it."

I turn her around and unzip her prom dress and pull it down over her shoulders toward her ass. "Out, out," I say. Her shoulders and back are covered with huge scars, they look like they're from both knives and burns—not from tonight, but from years and years of her father. Lots of kids are marked up, but this is pretty far out-there. She groans as the dress slides off her ass and into a pile on the floor; she's left wearing only her petticoats and lingerie. "Come on, step out of it," I prompt impatiently.

"I like you like this," I say to her, stepping into the dress. I bring it up to my hips, hand my jacket, holster, and shirt to Greg, and then pull the dress over my shoulders. It's heavily stained with barf and food and a little blood. The girl looks around in surprise and watches me put it on. It's tight as hell, but I'll live with it. "Zip me up?" I ask, turning around. She complies dumbly, and watches me walk over to Greg and his captive, who are laughing.

"You're a mess, honey," he says. "Didn't dinner agree with you?"

"I should have had the fish." I put the holster back on and then the jacket, tossing my shirt to the naked girl Greg is holding. "Here, don't say I never gave you anything." I pause to reload.

"Fuck you," she says, tossing the shirt on the floor, where it drapes across numerous other pieces of clothing, used rubbers, empty bottles, and various messes. We continue down the hallway, come still leaking out of my butt, and stop in front of room 717.

4

Piss is dripping off my lips, my cheeks, my eyebrows. God knows how long I've been in here. I didn't know that the entire senior class of Burns plus their dates had this much piss in them.

I'm on my back with my legs spread, wearing only the petticoats. The dress I ripped off long ago, it's lying in the corner looking like a dead terrier. I guess my dad is going to lose his deposit on it.

The chick I'm doing it with is squatting over me, inserting a travel-sized bottle of shampoo into my ass as I tip backward, legs like a TV aerial. My ass swallows it up greedily and she inserts the accompanying little bottle of conditioner. I yelp like a puppy as her fingernails inadvertently scratch my anus.

"Now out," she says.

I plant my feet on the floor and shit the little bottles out into her waiting hands. "Uucchhh!" I shout as the second one boinks out. We've been doing this for a while and my ass is getting pretty tired.

Some giggling couple comes in to check it out. They stand just inside the door, mouths agape. They're watching the two of us as well as the sixteen other chicks in the room, some of whom are lying in puddles seemingly unconscious, some of whom, like us, are fucking, some of whom—the most heavy-duty bottoms—are still on their knees as their boyfriends ordered, mouths open, waiting for that next trickle.

A chick over to the side who's fisting another chick snaps at the couple, "If you're not going to piss, then get the fuck out!" The guy bursts out laughing and we all reach for our knives and sneer, "Come a little closer and we'll give you something to laugh about."

Then a few guys come into the room and open their flies and pee on us. I turn my face upwards to get it because it's from Johnny. Not him personally but everything that happens to me tonight is from him because he wills it.

The guy who laughed finally gets his courage up and goes over to one of the most unconscious chicks curled up on the floor, I guess because she looks the least dangerous. He stands far away from her and as he pisses, his urine makes an arc through the air, spattering on her matted hair, her bare shoulders, her back with the bra still fastened. Maybe she's dead, I don't know.

The guy's girlfriend comes over to us and opens up her skirts and starts fingering herself while she pisses on us. This makes the piss fly everywhere like one of those crazy lawn-watering things. A low rhythmic guttural sound comes from her as she finishes: "Unh, uhn, uhn." Some orgasm. When she's finished she daintily wipes her fingers on her dress and looks askance at us and asks in a low, confidential voice, "Why are you doing this?" Then she hurries away with her date.

"Must be from another school," I tell my paramour, who is lazily circling my cunt mouth with her fingertips. Seems to be a break in the action; I guess those fucks broke the mood.

She looks at me and smiles, I like it. I ask how she wound up here. She says her boyfriend got drunk and passed out and she came in here on purpose. "I've always gotten off on degradation," she admits.

She suddenly leaves. I lie back, exhausted, wearing little. I only get to lie there for a moment before some people come in and pull me to my knees and do it in my face, then leave. They shut the door. It's suddenly quiet, and I reach my tongue out to catch the fresh piss that drips down my face. This is the best moment, the moment when I'm doing something because I want to, the reason Johnny brought me in here, not just to degrade me, but because he knows I frankly like it.

I lick my lips. I wouldn't mind a piece of chewing gum.

Then the door opens. Still on my knees, my tongue reaching to catch the piss that's dripping fresh from the tip of my nose, I see Johnny and Greg standing in the doorway. God, it's good to see them. I don't know who this naked chick is that they're pushing in before them, pushing down to the floor next to me—she snarls at them like a wildcat—but whatever they're bringing, it's always good.

"You look fetching," Lizza says to me, eyeing the dress I hijacked from the girl in the hall. She's stark naked and soaked with piss.

"Hold her, Lizza," I say. "She's a fighter," and laugh because that's what they said about my father at his funeral—total lie.

Lizza grabs the chick's wrists and holds on; if the girl struggles too much, she digs her nails in. "Better give it up," she advises. "Get with the program, as our Mr. Rikkles used to say.... What do you want with her?" she asks us.

"Oh, she's just a smartass," Greg says. "I thought a few minutes on her knees in here would help her attitude."

"Fuck you," the girl laughs, "I don't give a shit. All I want is to get fucked, I told you that."

"Right, *that's* it," I say, remembering. "She walked in on me and Greg and wanted to know if we were total faggots or if we could satisfy her pussy. Something like that."

Lizza is cracking up. "Baby," she laughs, "they *are* total faggots, and they *do* satisfy my pussy. You just don't realize," she adds, laughing.

"Can you get it up again?" Greg asks. "I'm pretty tired."

"Me too," I say. "I think you would have to make it interesting."

"God, what kind of orgy is this where you can't even get fucked!" grouses the girl.

Lizza smacks her. "I can see what these guys are talking about," Lizza says to her. "Why are you such a fucking grouch? Can't you see that these are, like, the hottest fucks in the world, and whatever they give you is going to be better than you ever had it? And that afterward—if you survive, that is—you won't be just some brown-haired chick in a bad mood, but you'll be better.... Oh, fuck you if you don't care."

"I know," Greg says brightly. "Keep holding her, whore," he says to Lizza. "Not you—" to the grouchy chick—"you're like an apprentice whore around here till you improve your attitude."

"God," she says with heavy irony.

"Look, it just provokes them," Lizza tells her.

Greg and I go into the bathroom. There are supplies in a little basket, little tubes of toothpaste, cologne, mouthwash; the shampoo and the conditioner are gone. Greg rummages through and comes up with a disposable plastic razor. "This should do the trick."

We go back into the room where a dozen piss-stained teenagers in various states of dress and consciousness still wait. "On all fours with her," he orders Lizza, who gets the girl around the throat, squeezing the carotid just enough to let her know she means business.

"Oh," the girl says.

Greg, wearing that leather thing, his gorgeous prick hanging down limp, stands over the girl as if he's getting ready for a horsey ride. I can see his butt tighten as he adjusts his stance. He looks over his shoulder to me and says, "Give it to her while I take care of her."

I kneel behind the girl and push fingers into her. "Unnhh," she grunts, thrusting back against my hand. "This more like what you had in mind?" I ask.

"Yes!" she snaps, pushing back, getting what she can.

Greg reaches down and cups her chin with his hand, forcing her head back. Lizza takes over with the chin hold, the other hand still on the chick's throat. Then Greg starts cutting her curly brown hair off with his knife.

"Ahhh!" she yells, but pushes back against my hand. I slide another finger in beside the three that're already there. "Ahhh!"

It takes a while to cut all the hair off. "Fuck, just fuck me," she pleads.

"My prick's getting hard, Greg, you're a genius."

"Thank me later," he grunts, slicing off another handful. He's like Han Solo struggling with the controls of the *Millennium Falcon*.

People are still coming in to piss. I direct a classmate to urinate on the chick's cunt as I finger-fuck her. She's pretty wet, but every little bit helps. The sight of piss getting directed at the captive chick's cunt completes my erection.

The girl now looks like Joan of Arc. "Fuck me, I don't care about my fucking hair," she grimaces, her mouth held closed by Lizza, who's still cupping her chin back.

"Better," Greg observes. Lizza snickers, "Let's get her head wet and soap it up."

We drag the chick into the bathroom; a lot of the fight has been taken out of her, but she still struggles, mostly to reach Lizza's mouth. "If that's the way you want it," Lizza snarls. Naked, she leaps into the shower with the chick and turns on the water. It steams around them.

Greg picks up the piece of soap from the sink and soaps his hands, then covers the girl's head with suds. "Keep her head out of the water, Lisa," he says.

"It's Lizza," she snaps, then sticks her tongue down the girl's throat again. I notice the girl has her fingers in Lizza's pussy. Standing in the steaming shower, they look just like actresses in a porn movie.

Greg takes the little disposable razor and starts shaving the girl's head. The girl breaks away from Lizza's mouth and says, "Fuck me!" like, haven't I told you enough times. Lizza crams her fingers into the girl's cunt. "No, with a prick," the girl insists.

"Shut up," Lizza says. "How can he fuck you when you're getting your head shaved." The little razor wasn't made for this kind of action and Greg has to work hard, but what's left of the hair gradually falls away. He keeps rinsing off the razor in the shower water. Halfway through, Lizza sticks the girl's head under the shower spray. She's half bald now. As Greg soaps up his hands and the girl's head again, I go next door, my erect prick sticking up under my dress like a tent pole, and get another razor. This one works faster. While he shaves, Lizza is working her hand gradually into the girl's cunt. Just as Greg finishes and shoves the girl's head under the water, Lizza slides her whole fist into the girl's cunt.

We lower the girl to her hands and knees as the water slides over them. The sight of Lizza fisting this completely bald girl is really something. "Now me," Lizza says, her arm working away. "Shave my head too."

They work around so that Greg can get at Lizza's head while she fists the girl. He soaps it up and starts hacking away with the little razor, but all he can really do with it is shave off, starting at the sides of the head and the back. "Never mind, just keep doing it," Lizza says. I see that somehow she has the knife that Greg used to cut the girl's long hair off with. She cuts the girl on the arm and the blood mixes with the water that's running over her. The girl squeaks but she seems to be lost in getting fucked and whatever she's high on, so that I don't think she really notices the pain.

I raise my skirts and Lizza turns her head and puts her mouth around my prick. "Deeper," I say. More blood runs. I fuck Lizza's mouth but it's not going to get me off. Greg has stopped trying to shave Lizza's head by now. I push him down on the floor and drag his body until I can get the best view of Lizza fucking and cutting the girl, then I push my prick deep in him. Unlubricated, he shouts in pain but I ignore him.

"Right before I come, I'll tell you," I gasp to Lizza.

"Yes."

I fuck Greg's ass steadily, gradually increasing the speed. He's moaning, his upper body sticking into the shower and the leather of his merry widow getting wet, the bloody water swirling beneath his body. He lowers his face into the stream to taste the blood, then raises his head and shows me the blood on his mouth. I fuck him harder, faster, the sight of blood turning me on more and more. Without someone whipping me or hitting my face or pulling on my tits, now I need the sight of blood to come.

"Closer," I bark out to my sister. She responds by making another slit in the girl's arm, so deep that the girl finally reacts and starts whimpering. Blood is streaming down into the shower stall. I focus on the dribbling, wish it to be more. Lizza doesn't wait for me to ask but cuts the girl again, all the while throwing her fist into the chick's cunt.

"Oh, god," the girl says. She is starting to tremble, probably from shock. Greg's moans combine with hers. He stretches his neck to the side, sinks his teeth into the girl's tit, like he's trying to bite off her nipple. I can feel his intestines spasming around my cock.

"Closer," I call out again. Now Lizza reaches down and cuts the girl's leg, a slicing cut across the calf as she kneels, hitting a vein. Blood rushes out of this new hole. I start to shake. "Oh, jesus."

I feel the orgasm gather itself in the pit of my guts like a sudden tornado. I have to come or it'll shake me apart.

"You fucking cunt, you bitch, you filthy whore," I say, meaning partly Greg and partly Lizza. "You fucking shit, I'm coming, do it now, do it now, do it now."

Lizza slashes the girl across the back and immediately red rushes out of there. I scream and begin shooting into Greg. Lizza slashes the girl again and again, the chick is screaming, I am screaming, and Lizza is maniacally hissing, "Fuck you, fuck you," at the girl she's knifing. Come hurtles out of my prick into Greg's guts.

"Hit me," I beg, only a few seconds left in my orgasm. Lizza tosses the knife away and drops the chick like a water balloon and slaps me across the face again and again. Another thrill starts in the center of my being and rushes out of my cock. "Aaauuugggghhhhhhhh," I grunt, the slaps like little explosions in my brain. I can't believe my orgasm is this good without me getting fucked too.

I slump to the floor and watch Lizza bend down and put her face to Greg's asshole as he shudders and convulses. She licks up my come as it comes trickling out.

On the way out of the room Lizza picks up her utterly degraded prom dress and sweats back into it somehow; wearing this filthy and torn-up dress, she looks like a refuge from a zombie movie.

Right before dawn everyone crowds into the elevators. Everyone has to be on the roof. The elevators are filled with the stink of piss and come and vomit; the floors are indescribable. Lizza is next to me, her eyes are wild. If it wasn't so packed in here, I could raise my arm to hit her, but I can hardly move. I bend over and bite her shoulder as hard as I can. Her breath is loud in the car; in fact, no one is speaking, all you can hear is breathing. We the survivors are gathering our energy for the final scene. I reach out my hand and the first thing it encounters is a messy piece of skin, which I stroke. I think that, if the chick we fucked in the shower survived, it might be nice to have her right here.

Behind me someone starts yelling, someone else starts moaning and comes. I can't even turn to see what's happening. The elevator arrives and we explode out into a service area just beneath the roof. It's almost as crowded here as in the elevator. I turn to look at the elevator doors closing and see a boy slumped on the floor, his chest freshly slashed in several places, panicking and trying to keep the blood that's everywhere from oozing out.

At the last moment I stop the elevator doors from closing. "Back!" I yell at Greg and Lizza as the adjacent elevator arrives and starts spilling people out. My two lovers catch up to me and pile into the now-empty elevator, empty except for the dying boy. I recognize him as a kid who lives on my block. He used to mow our lawn.

Without a word the three of us fall on the bleeding boy and start ripping him apart with our teeth. He has enough life in him to start screaming again. Greg is eating the guy's balls and prick, Lizza is tearing long strips of flesh away from his soft stomach, I am at his face, ripping it apart furiously. Each of us is screaming in our throats as we work, and tearing blindly with our hands. Lizza's fingernails tear open my own chest as she sticks her tongue into the knife wounds.

It's amazing to be eating the face of someone who's screaming. Once I've torn almost all of the loose part of his cheeks away, I spin around and shit into his still-moaning mouth. He starts choking but somehow he's still going. It's hard to kill someone.

The elevator is going down, down, down. I'm hard again. I stick my prick into the shit-filled cavern that used to be the guy's face, pumping my cock all the way down his throat. Now he finally starts to smother; he can't bite because all of his reflexes are making him gasp, wide open, for breath. His body convulses furiously as he smothers, and Greg and Lizza fight back, punching him with all their might. The guy's genitals are completely gone, with his crotch just a mass of blood and tissue. Finally he goes unconscious as the elevator stops in the lobby and the doors open.

People gape at us; we're absolutely soaked in blood. I look over at Lizza as she crouches over the body of the dead boy, looking like a wild maniac. Only a couple of dykes, who look too tough to let anything scare them, risk getting on the elevator with us. The doors close again.

Greg crawls over to Lizza's feet as she sits back against the wall of the elevator. Kneeling, Greg vomits blood and balls and pieces of penis on her feet, then licks them. She doesn't react, seems to be back in her trance.

At the seventh and subsequent floors, more people crowd onto the elevator. I don't bother to stand up; I feel invulnerable. Someone finds my head next to their crotch; they hold their penis out to me and piss in my face. I put my mouth around the spurting penis and drink.

When the elevator reaches the top again, we get out with the rest of our classmates and push our way up a metal stairway to the roof. It's not an open field; it's a maze of spaces between air-conditioning units, pipes, vents, and machinery sheds. Gravel covers the spaces between obstacles; compared to the hallways and rooms of the hotel, the roof seems clean. Around the edges is a wall about three feet high, topped with a railing.

The sky is growing light as we crowd into the spaces. I see a group of jocks approach a couple of girls, both of whom are stark naked, and take one. They hold her down and rape her while shouting unintelligible drunken phrases and "Go, go!" So predictable. It's only surprising because most of the drunks have passed out by now.

Most people congregate at the edge of the roof on the eastern side. They start tossing bottles and shoes and stuff off, leaning over the edge to see them strike the ground. The mood gets contagious and once people have run out of things to throw they start ripping off what's left of their clothing and toss that off, laughing.

Greg, Lizza, and I are wandering peacefully among the giant aluminum HVAC chimneys and roaring machinery and fucked-up people like we're at the mall. It's already hot outside; the Texas heat and humidity wake before dawn.

Lizza is clinging to Greg. She has one hand around his neck and the other on his ass and she's directing a stream of obscenities at him. "The three of us killed someone together, killed him for our fucking pleasure, I want to stick a knife blade up your ass, I want to make you hurt the way Johnny hurt you with his prick, I'd like to cut you open and see your guts start spilling out and piss in the hole I made. Fucking faggot, get your prick hard for me, stick it in my mouth, but fuck Johnny first, I want to taste his shit, I want to suck it off your prick. What makes you think you're going to survive until sunrise, motherfucker? Tell me now how you used to fuck your little sister, tell me or I'll kill you."

Greg is gasping because she's sticking her fingers up his butthole and alternately tightening and loosening her grip around his throat. Both of them look over at me. "I can see what you like about him," she smiles.

I see four of the people, the acid queens, from the limo: three boys and the slave. The boys are on their knees in the gravel, still mostly dressed, digging frantically with their hands and moaning; I guess the wide-open spaces of the roof freak them out after the confinement of the hotel. The girl is standing near them, wearing nothing but a silk blouse, not doing much except idly digging her nails into her thighs. She has long, scabbing cuts on her legs and back, and her red hair is matted and still bears signs of the food fight, but compared to other people, she's in pretty good shape.

If I had anything left, I could get hard for her, but after the scene in the elevator I feel transparent. I've lost track of my orgasms, of the people I killed, of my clothing. I practically don't care what happens to me; if the jocks rushed me now, I wouldn't even struggle.

Right about that time the first person gets thrown off the roof. I don't even really see it, I just see a scurrying of movement. There's some screaming, from both the victim and the aggressors. I think it's those jocks. The trouble with them is that, duh, they're big enough to really tackle somebody and throw them off. The way I feel, so exhausted and passive and yet completely alert, I'd make a perfect victim, and in a way I wouldn't mind; I would just prefer that Greg and Lizza did it to me than a bunch of jocks.

There's no room at the roof's edge because everyone's lined the rail to see people fly, so the three of us sit down a ways back from the crowd, with a view of everyone's asses. I kiss Greg, I want to get lost in his mouth that tastes like the boy's flesh he's just eaten and vomited. But after a while of this, Lizza pulls me away from him and slaps me hard. She can see me sinking into passivity, and it's too dangerous. I think, as she wallops me across the face again and again, it's really nice of her to take care of me.

"That was in the morning," Greg says, now starting to breathe hard as he strokes into my girlfriend's anus. "For the rest of the day, and in fact for the rest of the weekend, every time we saw each other in the house, she would whisper into my ear, 'Fuck me again, why aren't you fucking me right now?'" and I would get instantly hard. We didn't even do anything for the rest of the weekend, we didn't have to, all we did was this thing where she would whisper to me about fucking her. It drove me fucking nuts."

Lizza turns from my cock. Because she's on her back, her legs now drawn up on either side of Greg's ears, she can look him in the face. "Fuck her now, you bastard," she says. "Fuck your little sister's ass, fuck me, I'll be your sister, you're fucking your little sister's asshole and I'm looking right into your eyes, just like that time, and saying fuck me, fuck me, fuck your sister's cunt."

The great thing about this scene is that Greg doesn't even have a sister. He picked up on her cue and she picked up on his story and became a character in it and they're fucking beautifully, so beautifully, I love them now as I watch them doing it. I want to be her getting fucked, I want to be him fucking her, I want to be his little sister bleeding on her brother's prick. Even just watching, I'm completely connected with their sex and their stories and completely turned on, although it feels like I'll never come again.

"Oh god, it's starting to feel really good," Lizza grunts. "Oh god, it's feeling really good. Oh fuck. Just keep doing it."

Greg leans over and kisses me. And kisses me.

And nothing else happens except him fucking her without coming, her moaning and shaking and finally crying and still saying, "Don't stop fucking me. Don't stop fucking me in the ass. Oh jesus christ, don't stop fucking my fucking shitty ass." On and on.

Finally, we go down the stairs. The fire department is hosing everything down, it's pretty disgusting, but Lizza manages to find a piece of someone's femur and hide it underneath her dress. We get into someone's car, it's the red convertible of somebody who's been killed sometime between the time they dropped their car off and now.

We get into the front seat, me, Lizza, Greg. We blast down the freeway in the rising sun. It takes two hours to get to the coast. Lizza drags the leg bone she's stolen up out of her bloody piss-smeared skirts, and rams it home, fucks herself with it as she begs me to assure her the bone belongs to someone I've killed—not just anyone, but someone I've killed for her—and if she can fuck herself with the very marrow of the bones of someone who died for her pleasure, then she'll get off.

The skirts fly into the air and are blown away. She's totally naked in the red convertible, sitting on the long black leather bench seat between us, glowing in the sunlight.

AFTERWORD

With one exception, all these stories were started at various times during the 1990s and finished during the winter of 2000–2001. They represent an unusual slice of my work, and I would like to say a few things about some themes that kept popping up.

"Prom" is a story I started in 1990. I wrote most of the story in one sitting, on a sunny summer Sunday afternoon, under the influence. Then I spent time over the next few years cleaning it up, adding material, and generally polishing.

Now, I used to be very high-functioning on certain substances (which in any case I don't do anymore). But it's still a wonder how it was possible for me to concentrate enough to put down anything remotely coherent. In this case they actually made me concentrate while at the same time freeing my inhibitions—a good combination when it comes to writing porn. Without this aid, I don't know if the violent images in "Prom" would have come to the surface, or if I would have had the guts to write them down.

Certainly they came as a surprise to me and my friends, and although I don't think I've lost any friends over stuff I've put into sex stories, I still have to wonder where all the violent stuff came from.

Well, to start with, there are all the violent images I've seen on TV and in films, not to mention my avid reading of the Old Testament and the Marquis de Sade. I've seen little violent pornography per se, but how much difference is there between violent porn and, say, the movie *Alien*, where the monster crawls down someone's throat, incubates inside his abdomen, and then bursts out through his chest—as many have observed, a sequence that is little more than a demonic pregnancy.

Even without these media images, people seem to have the capacity to sexualize almost anything or anybody they really care about, subconsciously if not consciously. I think that's why almost everyone has dreams about sex with their parents, teachers, coworkers, clergy, or others they aren't supposed to have sex with.

So these images and desires are, for better or worse, inside me. That I document them—even celebrate them—by writing them down doesn't mean I do these things or really want to do them, any more than the writer of *Alien* wants to have a monster incubating in his abdomen. I think documenting these sexual, violent images is a way of saying, "Hey look at this—look what's under this rock—isn't that weird?"

The setting of "Prom" is also a starting place. The American suburb depicted in this story, and in "Cousin," is an evocation of the purgatory in which I spent my high school years, a bleak collection of housing developments and strip malls situated halfway between Houston and Galveston, Texas. I find this sterile environment, like a blank canvas where anything can happen, a perfect setting for perversion.

As for the characters, teenagers are these repressed bundles of hormones and delusions of immortality. They're not supposed to have sex or do anything, but of course they do. (Not that any of these teenage stories describe my actual experience, or even second-hand knowledge; when I was a teenager I was a complete dork and utterly clueless about what the other teens were probably doing all around me.) That's the theme of all these suburb stories: that behind the split-level beige façade, people are acting out their sickness and repression big-time. Not so unbelievable after all, come to think of it.

Readers of my first book, *Too Beautiful*, will notice that the main female character in "Prom" shares a name with the title character of the story "Lizza" in that book. Are they the same person? In a way. In both stories, Lizza is the sexually ravenous suburban kid whose desire transgresses the boundaries of her gender, the law, and sometimes anatomy. Drawing a straight line from the sixteen-year-old Lizza in "Prom" to the nineteen-year-old one in "Lizza" is not as easy; "Lizza" was written first, and "Prom" is not really meant to be a prequel. Rather, Lizza represents, to me, an archetype of the sexually powerful teenager.

In "Cousin," as well as any of the other stories where incest is described—well, actually, for all the stories in this book—I must reiterate the classic disclaimer about the persons and events having no resemblance, etc. Although when I read "Cousin" at a holiday-themed erotica reading (Thomas Roche's annual "Xmas Sucks" event, which usually takes place in a freezing San Francisco basement about a week before Christmas), a listener commented, "I grew up in Tacoma, and it is just like that."

"Ordinary Story" is the one in which the time gap between its start and its completion was probably the longest. It started out as a standard boy–boy story; I wanted to write another one as good as the title story of *Too Beautiful*. But I bogged down in the middle, and when I picked it up again almost ten years later, I cut out half of what I'd done, which ventured into all kinds of stuff like drag that I don't really know much about. Once I introduced the Pamela character, I just sort of let her cut loose. I really like the way the story has turned out; I was grinning to myself as I wrote the last lines. For Pamela's voice, I imagined that of Cheryl Trykv, a writer I heard on the radio show *This*

American Life. (If you want to hear her voice, go to its website, www.thislife.org, and listen to the May 15, 1998, show, the segment "Paw Paw for Jesus." It's an amazing voice, full of spit 'n' vinegar.)

"Ordinary Story" is dedicated to a girlfriend, Stephanie Kulick, who was killed in 1999 in a car crash. She was nothing like the Pamela character, but she would have loved the ending where the guy has to admit he's a "big bisexual fag." Stephanie was a worker and union organizer at the Lusty Lady, the setting of the documentary *Live Nude Girls Unite*, and can be glimpsed in that film.

"Incest" is the story that I have the hardest time discussing, because it deals with a girl who's really underage—not just 16 but 11—and our culture has a very hard time looking at minors and sex, even if they are mere characters in a story. Almost everything I write about this piece (for example, to observe that incest has been a common theme of pornography for hundreds of years) ends up sounding like a rationalization or an excuse about why it's really okay for me to write about what I have written about. In a moment I'll talk about this issue of writing about something that one "shouldn't" write about, and that reasoning applies to this story and to writing porn in general. About "Incest," I'll just make a couple of observations.

For one thing, it's only sometimes true that, while I'm writing a sex scene, I'm aroused; it's even more rare for me to become aroused by the same material once I've edited and worked on it. That said, the first scene of "Incest" is one that never fails to turn me on. The combination of the incest situation and the ages of the characters and the little girl urinating strike a powerful erotic chord in me.

The other observation is that this story ends at a point where it could obviously be continued and turned into a conventional porn novel, but I chose not to do so—at least, for now. I can't figure out how to give it enough of a twist to make it really interesting. The most interesting part of erotica with an incest theme is, of course, the "education" of the innocent. Once you get past that part—which is where this story ends—it becomes pretty standard heterosexual porn.

"How I Adore You" was begun later than all these, although after writing the first scene I didn't know where to take the story. I wrote about three different middles and one lousy ending, and then sat on the piece for more than a year. Finally I realized all I had to do was let the two characters confront each other. They work out some issues I was dealing with at the time, having to do with setting and breaking physical and emotional boundaries between lovers. Aside from the farcical scene in the suburban lesbian bar in the middle of the story, this is one of the most serious pieces in the book, and it means a lot to me.

It's also the only piece in my body of work where there are no boys at all. Given the fact that I'm a male, it's not surprising that most of my stories are about guys. And while I don't intentionally write "bisexual erotica," the bisexuality of most of my characters is apparent. In stories where there are men and women, everybody usually ends up doing everybody else, somehow; it's a challenge for me not to make all my characters bisexual, in behavior if not in self-definition. This is not because I have some kind of bisexual agenda, but because I believe that most people have the capacity to have sex with both men and women, and, given the right situation, would do so.

But in "How I Adore You" I took the men out altogether. Yet some people would say that a story written by a man can never completely have all the men taken out of it, which is certainly true. This brings up the issue of whether or not it's okay for a man to write about lesbian sex. Faux-lesbian erotica written or photographed by men has, of course, been a staple of porn for many years. Without attempting to analyze why this is, and knowing that it bugs the shit out of a lot of lesbians, I want to say why I go ahead and do it anyway.

I write porn because it turns me on to write about sex, and to express in a different medium the same feelings and desires I express in bed. Writing it down solidifies my desires, commemorates them, makes them live outside me. Writing allows me to capture the images that are so fleeting during arousal, long enough for me to examine them and wonder what they mean and where they came from. Writing about these images and desires also tells the people who are close to me, really close to me, who I am and what's inside me.

For these reasons, I don't want to limit what I can write about—as I did back in the '70s, when my sexual expression was very politically correct, and I never would have imagined either being rough with a sexual partner or writing about it. Getting over those self-imposed limits has improved my sex and my writing, and I'm not going to stop now. At the same time, I'm obviously not a lesbian (nor am I one of those silly men who claim they are "male lesbians"), and no doubt there are many things I'll never know or understand about the dynamics of lesbian desire or what women do together. Given that limitation, "How I Adore You" is still, I believe, an emotionally convincing story and good erotica.

The last story to be written was "Trick," and it's as monosexual as "How I Adore You"—no girls allowed! After the sequences between the narrator and Cary and his "daddy," a trio of porn stars suddenly burst on the scene, getting in the way and breaking up the warmth between the narrator and Cary. I know that some readers who are really into the Daddy thing will be pissed at the way these clowns break up the scene and preclude hot, Daddy-ridden sex for the rest of the night—especially after I teased people in my first book with "Daddy's Play Party," a story that promises to be about hot leather sex but is not. But after a few pages, I'd had about as much of Daddy as I could take. Frankly, I can't write about leather sex without its turning into some kind of farce. So on come the porn gods, and the narrator goes off in their big *machina*.

"Trick" is a little sad, as are many of my sex stories. Maybe after AIDS it's not possible to write about sex without including equal portions of grief and ecstasy, love and loss. Without this awareness of—let's say it—death, a sex book becomes a sterile Disneyland of the senses, like those *Star Trek* episodes where they beam down to a planet where everyone's running around in G-strings being polyamorous. I don't live in a world like that; no one does anymore. In the sense that people are still a little shell-shocked after the loss of so many friends and lovers, not to mention the loss of the Edenic queer sexuality of the '70s, San Francisco is like a battlefield after a battle. The survivors are stronger, and we go on to love each other. True, there are holes in the fabric of queer San Francisco—missing people, absent art, great loves that will never be. But it is as much in their memory, and in honor of the many battles they fought—for dignity, for human rights, and to free everyone from the straitjacket of straight American sexuality—as it is to fulfill our own desires, that we try to be filthy, dirty sluts for the twenty-first century.

About the Author

Mark Pritchard is the author of *Too Beautiful and Other Stories* (Cleis Press, 2001), a new, expanded edition of his first collection of erotic stories, originally published by Masquerade Books in 1999. He was coeditor and publisher of the early '90s sex-and-politics zine *Frighten the Horses*. He is a former San Francisco Sex Information volunteer and a former member of Queer Nation and the Street Patrol. He lives in Bernal Heights, San Francisco, where he is working on a novel about the Rat Pack. He can be contacted at toobeaut@yahoo.com.